AROUND THE WORLD IN 80 DAYS

BY
DAVID BENULLO AND DAVID GOLDSTEIN

BASED ON THE SCREENPLAY BY
MICHAEL WEISS AND DAVID BENULLO
& DAVID GOLDSTEIN

ADAPTED FROM THE NOVEL BY
JULES VERNE

HYPERION BOOKS FOR CHILDREN

NEW YORK

1 ❖ In Which a Robbery Takes Place

PHILEAS FOGG HAD THE SAME DREAM every night. He soared through the sky like a bird, surrounded by billowy, white clouds. "It is possible!" he would cry, delirious with joy. "Man can fly!"

THUMP! Suddenly a chicken, dressed in a tuxedo, appeared on the wing of Fogg's fantastic flying machine.

"A chicken?" Phileas gaped. "Unthinkable! Even if a flightless bird could ascend this far into the stratosphere, the lack of oxygen would make breathing nearly impossible! Also, he's wearing a tuxedo! This must be . . ."

RI-I-I-I-ING! sounded his alarm clock.

". . . A dream," said Phileas foggily, as he sat up.

Someday, Phileas thought, I will fly through the heavens and it won't be a dream. Someday . . .

CLANNNNGGGGG!!!!!! An earsplitting ring filled the air along London's Threadneedle Street. It wasn't the boom of Big Ben—London's most famous timepiece—announcing the new hour. Nor was it the morning melody of Westminster Abbey's church bells chiming. It was the very unmusical clanging of a burglar alarm. The Bank of England had just been robbed!

A giant fortress of stone and steel, the Bank of England had massive vaults filled with gold bars and priceless artifacts, as well as much of Queen Victoria's immense fortune. It was believed to be the safest and most secure building in the world.

CLAAAANNNNNNG!

But sometimes *seeing* was believing.

A flood of bobbies—London policemen—charged down the street blowing whistles and waving billy clubs. They crowded the bank's entrance, blocking what they believed to be the robber's only means of escape.

But again, sometimes seeing was believing.

CRASH! The bank's second-floor window erupted in a shower of broken glass. The bank robber smashed through, riding a valuable red velvet couch to the ground. It landed on the street with a loud thud, the legs snapping under the impact. Dust and feathers billowed up in a huge cloud. Suddenly the valuable red velvet couch wasn't so valuable anymore.

The cloud of couch dust quickly cleared, revealing a Chinese man with a thick mustache and beard.

Wiping dust and feathers from his face, he patted the leather pouch strapped to his side, sprang to his feet like a tiger, and raced down the street.

The stunned and confused bobbies gathered their bearings and chased the Chinese man into a neighboring building.

WHOOSH! The Chinese man slid open a window and backed out onto the street, utterly confusing the bobbies. Apparently, they were familiar only with the more traditional bank robber-types, who preferred to use doors for their getaways.

Looking for a quick exit, the Chinese man hopped a ride on the back of a passing horse-drawn carriage and disappeared from sight.

The robber was in luck. Whereas your usual robber/carriage-hopper might have found himself landing in the middle of a shipment of pitchforks or a sack of horse manure, this particular bank robber landed on a carriage belonging to one of the best tailors in London, and it was filled with new clothes from the tailor's shop.

The carriage traveled a few blocks before the Chinese man hopped off the back, looking completely different.

He was now clean-shaven, his long, flowing hair pulled back in a neat ponytail. He adjusted his dapper, new suit, and flipped on his brand-new top hat. The baffled bobbies ran right past him, continuing their search for a *bearded* bank robber.

Figuring his disguise would soon be discovered, the robber scrambled up a nearby tree, disappearing from view. He was safe, for a moment. But he knew the hunt wasn't over. The bobbies would search long and hard for the person who had robbed the Bank of England.

As he took a moment to catch his breath, a loud rattling filled the air. He looked down to the courtyard below.

There clanked a giant contraption filled with tubes, rails, and other gadgets, including a giant, belching steam engine.

The man standing next to the device was almost as strange as the contraption itself. Phileas Fogg, never one to waste valuable inventing time on grooming or appearance, had a wild mane of unkempt, black hair and large goggles that magnified his intense gaze. He resembled a giant, hairy bug. The Chinese man couldn't help but smile.

2 ❖ IN WHICH PHILEAS HIRES A NEW VALET

PACING NERVOUSLY IN HIS COURTYARD, Phileas Fogg was too preoccupied with his thoughts to notice the robber hiding in the tree above him. Phileas was certain he was on the verge of a great scientific breakthrough—the first successful test of a steam-powered jet pack.

Resembling a giant vacuum cleaner, the pack was strapped to the back of Phileas's aged French valet, Jean Michel, who was himself strapped to a rig that looked like a small roller coaster. Jean Michel squirmed uncomfortably.

"It is time for the light of science to dispel the darkness of myth and superstition!" Phileas declared. "Man can break the fifty-mile-per-hour speed barrier without disrupting his internal organs."

"Disrupted organs!" cried Jean Michel, dismayed by the notion of his organs being altered in any way.

"We will make history," Phileas cried. "Or we will die trying!"

"Die?" repeated Jean Michel, his panic rising.

"I'm just being honest!" said Phileas.

"That's it!" declared Jean Michel. He unstrapped himself from the crazy contraption, his fingers fumbling nervously at the buckles. Rising to his feet, he pulled Phileas's homemade crash helmet from his skull. "I can endure preparing your toast at precisely eighty-two degrees, your bathwater at ninety-four degrees . . ."

"Ninety-six," Phileas corrected.

Jean Michel glared at Phileas. "But I refuse to be shot at, catapulted, or electrocuted, or to have my internal organs disrupted any longer!"

"The electrocution wasn't my fault," Phileas said. "You refused to wear rubber underpants!"

"I *quit*!" screamed Jean Michel, shoving the crash helmet into Phileas's arms before storming off . . . just as all of Phileas's valets had done before him.

As a rule, valets were well trained in the skills of managing a household. But Phileas had not yet found one willing to tolerate the rigors of testing his inventions.

"Is there no man brave enough to be my valet?" cried Phileas in despair.

Watching from his hiding spot in the tree, the amused robber was startled by the sound of a branch snapping. He tumbled from the tree in a rain of leaves, landing directly in front of an equally startled Phileas.

"Who are you?" a surprised Phileas exclaimed.

The robber's mind scrambled for an answer— and found one.

"I'm your new valet!" he replied, desperate not to be tossed back onto the streets, where the police were searching for him.

"I must commend the valet service for their impeccable foresight," Phileas marveled. He looked more closely at the muscular Chinese man standing before him. "But they know I only accept French valets."

"Oh, yes! *Oui!*" said the quick-thinking robber. "I come from a long line of French valets . . . on my father's side. Very, very French. My mother is Chinese."

On an ordinary day, a suspicious Phileas might have questioned the man further. But at that particular moment, the opportunity for a historic scientific breakthrough was the only thing on his mind. "Are you willing to risk your life to change the laws of physics as we know them?" he asked.

The bank robber wasn't worried about the laws of physics. He *was* worried about the laws of England—and the bobbies who enforced the law were now combing the area in pursuit of him.

"Yes!" the robber answered. "I can sing, too!"

"Excellent," Phileas remarked, wondering why the French-Chinese man thought his singing skills would come in handy. "Now, put on this crash . . . I mean, *safety* helmet."

The robber grabbed the helmet, pulling it over his head just as a pair of bobbies rushed past him. Phew! The helmet was a perfect disguise!

Phileas happily strapped the bank robber–turned–valet–turned–guinea pig onto the roller-coaster contraption and showed him how to operate the throttle to increase the machine's speed.

As the powerful steam engine coughed to life, the valet suddenly realized something. "How do I stop?" he yelled over the roar of the engine.

Having no good answer to that rather important safety question, Phileas pointed to his ears helplessly. "Sorry! I can't hear you!" He then gave his new valet an encouraging thumbs-up, signaling the start of the experiment.

The valet hit the throttle, and the jet pack erupted with a burst of energy. In a flash, he was rocketing along the small track that wound its way through the courtyard. It took all of his considerable strength just to hold on.

Phileas, closely monitoring the gauges from his control post, was thrilled. "Twenty-five miles per hour, and the pressure's stable!" he cried. He grabbed the megaphone perched in front of him and yelled out to his new assistant. "We need more speed!"

The valet nodded and pushed the throttle to its limit. He blasted along the track even faster. The track rattled loudly, the metal shaking and straining against the speed of the jet pack.

Phileas excitedly kept track of the speed as it climbed. "Forty-seven! Forty-eight! Forty-nine!" Finally, the gauge reached fifty miles per hour. "*Eureka!* We've done it!"

Phileas was ecstatic. His experiment was a success! But his excitement was sadly short-lived.

The track rattled madly, jarred by the intense vibrations of the circling jet pack. A bolt that held the track together slipped free, creating a makeshift ramp off which the jet pack—and the valet—were rocketed into the air. Pack and rider soared out of the courtyard, shaving the tops of the hedges as they cleared the fence.

Phileas couldn't believe his eyes. He raced after his new assistant, following the pack's erratic course through the elegant Savile Row section of London.

Nearby, two policemen stopped their search, frustrated by their inability to catch the man who had robbed the Bank of England.

"We've lost him, sir," the young bobby confessed to his sergeant.

"We'll find him, lad," the experienced officer responded confidently. "Just keep your eyes open for anything unusual."

Neither of them noticed the jet pack—carrying the very man they were searching for—fly past behind them, bouncing off the cobblestone street. The valet was knocked about like a human pinball, and sent startled pedestrians scattering in every direction.

Chasing his new valet through the streets, Phileas tried to reassure the terrified pedestrians by greeting them casually. "Good morning!" he cried cheerily. "I'm looking for a man wearing a steam turbine . . ."

"*Watch out!*" yelled the valet to two men transporting a large painting of a woman. But it was too late. The valet ripped through the back of the picture, his head jut out the front so that it appeared as though he were wearing the dress of the woman in the painting.

The valet careened into a lamppost—*CLANG!* It vibrated wildly from the impact, a large, safety helmet-shaped dent left in its middle. Thanks to the safety helmet, the valet's head would survive. The lamppost would not.

Phileas rushed over to his dazed valet. "Well done! We've broken the human speed record!"

The bank robber wobbled to his feet, fumbling to remove his helmet. "Good-bye, sir," he said. "It's been very nice *valeting* for you."

"Wait!" Phileas shouted in desperation. "With you as my brave valet, I can test *all* of my inventions." He marveled at the possibilities. "Would you be willing to wear rubber underpants?"

The robber swayed, still reeling from the ricocheting ride. Rubber underpants? What was this man talking about? But the shrill report of a nearby police whistle made him reconsider. . . .

"I'll take the job!" he said.

Phileas beamed. "Splendid! I can't wait to present my results to the Royal Academy!"

Phileas hoped his findings would impress the distinguished members of the Royal Academy of Science and he would finally be granted membership. As a Royal Academy Certified Scientist, Phileas would be able to introduce his many inventions to a group of experts—and then, possibly, to the entire world!

3 ❖ AT THE ROYAL ACADEMY OF SCIENCE

AS DIRECTOR OF THE ROYAL ACADEMY, Lord Kelvin was supposed to encourage new developments in science. Instead, he preferred to use his power to encourage new developments in his bank account.

Kelvin stole credit for any scientific ideas that could earn him money. If a scientist accused him of stealing, he made sure to ruin the person's good name and destroy his career. The crooked lords of the academy with whom Kelvin surrounded himself were all too happy to help him with his evil schemes as long as they were financially rewarded as well.

The scientist who made Kelvin and his associates most nervous was the smartest and most noble of them all—Phileas Fogg himself. Kelvin and the other lords had little respect for Phileas or for his silly dreams of using science to benefit mankind.

As Phileas and his new valet busied themselves with breaking the world speed record, Kelvin stood outside the Royal Academy Hall and spoke to a mass of all-too-trusting British citizens. Each day, Lord Kelvin gave a new speech, mocking another great scientific breakthrough, ensuring that England and its people would never benefit from these brilliant ideas. Today's target of ridicule was a brilliant French scientist named Louis Pasteur.

"Be on the lookout for Louis Pasteur. He is a dangerous madman!" Kelvin said as he held up the man's portrait. "He has attempted to convince the Academy that the most effective method of preventing a deadly disease is through a ludicrous concept called a vaccine, whereby—please try and contain your laughter—a man is *injected* with a disease in order to *prevent* it!" Kelvin burst into laughter. The crowd tittered naively.

Although Pasteur was correct and his medical breakthrough would someday save countless lives,

Lord Kelvin wanted to make certain that nobody in England took his ideas seriously.

Colonel Kitchner, chief of Scotland Yard—the name for the London police department—appeared next to the podium. "Sir, I have an urgent announcement for you," he whispered, nervously rattling the telegram he clutched.

"Don't just stand there, man," an irritated Kelvin barked. "Read it!"

Kitchner reluctantly proceeded: "'It is with great distress that Scotland Yard announces that the Bank of England has been robbed.'"

The crowd gasped.

Kelvin immediately took Kitchner inside his private office, slamming the doors behind him.

"My stolen jade Buddha—*stolen*?" Kelvin shouted. "You assured me that the Bank of England was impenetrable!"

Just days before the bank robbery, a priceless jade Buddha had been stolen from China and given to Kelvin as a bribe. Now a mysterious bank robber had stolen it back from right under Kelvin's nose.

Kelvin, furious beyond belief, grabbed everything within sight, heaving it all—pens, pencils, quills, paperweights—at the poor, beleaguered Kitchner, who took refuge behind a nearby chair. "Lord Salisbury," Kelvin ranted, turning to one of his henchmen. "Contact General Fang and inform her that our arrangement has become null and void! No Buddha, no deal!"

Suddenly they heard a woman's voice. "To forgo your obligation would be dishonorable, Lord Kelvin."

"A woman," gasped Lord Salisbury. "In the Royal Academy!"

Women weren't ordinarily allowed in the Royal Academy—but General Fang was no ordinary woman. Tall and intimidating, with the dark stare of a killer and frightfully long blades on the ends of her fingernails, this ruthless Chinese warlord was not afraid of anything. By her side were two of her Black Scorpion agents, identifiable by the scorpion tattoos on their biceps.

General Fang stalked over to Lord Kelvin. "The jade Buddha was successfully delivered by us to the Bank of England," she hissed.

Lord Kelvin wasn't scared of Fang. He had the power to give her what she wanted—the British military's help in taking over a part of China that

Fang was unable to capture by herself. "Until the jade Buddha is back in my possession," he informed her, "you and your 'cause' will receive no British military assistance whatsoever."

"My agents will retrieve the jade Buddha once again, Lord Kelvin," she told him furiously. "This time, do not let it slip through your fingers." She flashed her fingernail blades—sending shivers down the lords' spines.

As Fang turned to leave, Lord Kelvin furiously snatched a sharp-pointed quill pen from his desk and threw it at her. With lightning speed, she whirled and caught the quill in midair, firing it right back at him. The lords cowered in fear as the projectile soared across the room, striking a portrait of Lord Kelvin himself, right between the eyes! Then, in a flash, she was gone.

Now, even Lord Kelvin was rattled. But there was another woman who scared him even more than General Fang—Queen Victoria. If the queen found out that Lord Kelvin had plans to give British military assistance to Fang in exchange for the valuable Buddha, Kelvin would certainly lose his position as the director of the Royal Academy. And if Kelvin lost his job, he would also lose all of his power and money—basically, everything he cared about in the world. Kelvin had to cover up the robbery of the jade Buddha, somehow.

"Tell the newspapers that a fortune in gold, currency, and precious jewels has been stolen from the Bank of England," he ordered Colonel Kitchner. "We must not let anyone know about the jade Buddha—least of all, the queen."

4 ❖ IN WHICH PASSEPARTOUT NAMES HIMSELF AND TOURS FOGG MANSION

PHILEAS FOGG'S MANSION was a sight to behold. His new valet had certainly never seen anything like it. In fact, nobody who got a good look at it— and the house attracted plenty of stares—knew what to make of the residence.

What had once been an ordinary mansion had been transformed into a public eyesore with its bizarre metal domes, huge windmill, and rubber conveyer belts running in and out of the house.

As peculiar as the house appeared from the outside, the inside was even stranger—though not to Phileas, who showed his new valet around with pride. "My wind-powered pulley system supplies the house with fresh air," he explained. "Kitchen items are to be placed on the white belt, blue is for laundry."

He motioned to a series of gears and rotors. "This supplies the house with a running current of electricity."

The valet had never heard of such a thing. "E-lec-tri-cit-y," he said, trying out the word.

Phileas handed over a complicated schedule that mapped out every minute of his every day. It was Phileas's valet's responsibility to see that everything ran according to that schedule.

"I must live my life with total efficiency to maximize my inventing capacity," Phileas explained. It was then that Phileas realized he still did not know his new valet's name.

The problem was, neither did the valet. He couldn't give his real name—Lau Xing—which was obviously Chinese. Phileas thought that he was French. He needed a French name . . . and fast.

The valet looked out the window, catching sight of a pair of bobbies still doggedly looking for the bank robber. They had stopped a foreign man, who was showing them his passport. That gave the valet an idea.

"My name is Passport . . ." he said. Then, realizing that that name didn't sound French, he added, "too."

"Passepartout," Phileas said. "A peculiar name."

"Thank you, Mr. Phileas Fogg," replied Passepartout pointedly.

Phileas led Passepartout into his darkened laboratory and whistled, triggering the activation of dozens of lights.

Passepartout was amazed. The lightbulb was still a new invention, and he had never seen one. "Bottled light . . . a miracle!" he said.

"Hardly," Phileas said. "Just undiscovered science from an American named Thomas Edison."

"It turns on with a whistle?" Passepartout asked, whistling in amazement—inadvertently causing the lights to go out.

"Please don't do that," Phileas instructed. He whistled, and the room lit up once again. "It was going to be a clap," he explained, "but I feel my hands are put to far better use working on important things, like this."

Phileas pointed at a huge block of metal adorned with numerous pistons and gears.

"You invented this?! Unbelievable!" Passepartout

exclaimed, clearly impressed . . . if a little confused. "What is it?"

"It's an internal combustion engine," Phileas bragged. "I didn't invent it, but I did find a way to run it on a new source of fuel: kidney beans!"

Phileas poured a can of beans into the gizmo and turned it on. The sound was deafening. The pistons pumped and unleashed an odorous gas. Phileas quickly turned it off. "Pity, I haven't found a use for it. It has the power of one hundred horses."

"Why not use it instead of a horse?" suggested Passepartout.

"Interesting idea . . ." said Phileas, wondering why that thought had never occurred to him.

Passepartout picked up an object that looked like a cane.

"Be careful!" said Phileas.

"Is this dangerous?" asked Passepartout. His fingers brushed the cane's ivory handle, accidentally hitting a button that caused an umbrella to pop open from the cane's end.

"Only if you are superstitious," said Phileas. He took the cane from Passepartout, retracting the umbrella and putting the item away carefully.

Passepartout couldn't help noticing a giant,

winged contraption suspended from the ceiling. He approached it, fascinated.

"I see your eye is drawn to what I hope will one day be my crowning achievement," Phileas stated proudly.

"A giant moth?" said Passepartout.

"It's a flying machine."

"It can fly?"

"Yes," said Phileas confidently. "Well, no," he said, correcting himself. "Not yet . . . But one day, it will transport people through the air, perhaps over entire oceans."

Impressed, Passepartout let out a little whistle. Instantly, the lights went out. "Oops," he said.

The tour was over.

Phileas collected his charts and data, excited at the thought of presenting his results to the Royal Academy. The distraction gave Passepartout the opportunity to slip away and write an important telegram in secret.

Dear Father, Passepartout wrote. *I have taken back what was stolen from us. I will find the fastest way back to China to make our village safe once again.* Reaching gently into his leather pouch, Passepartout removed a gleaming jade statue of

Buddha. The object sparkled almost magically in the light. Nothing would stop Passepartout from returning the precious object to its rightful place.

Phileas's voice erupted through a funnel on the wall, startling Passepartout. His hands went into spasms, sending the Buddha tumbling into the air; Passepartout snatched it just before it crashed to the floor.

"Departure for the Royal Academy of Science is in two minutes!" Phileas declared. "Prepare my urban transport device!"

Passepartout was confused. *Urban transport—?*

"The shoes with little wheels on them," Phileas clarified.

Soon, Passepartout raced through the streets, running hard after Phileas. As well as ensuring his employer's safety, Passepartout's job was to apologize to the people Phileas nearly ran down with his wheeled shoes.

To most members of the Royal Academy, Phileas Fogg was merely an annoyance. To others, however, he was impressive.

"I have just heard that Phileas Fogg is building a flying machine!" said Sutton, Lord Kelvin's assistant. "Just *think* how it will revolutionize travel."

"Yes, just *think* of a wonderful world where everyone travels around in marvelous little flying machines . . ." Kelvin sneered. *"Instead of on the railways we own!"*

Just then, the doors to the Royal Academy spilled open, and Phileas rolled into the room, instructing Passepartout to stand alongside the other valets present.

Noticing Phileas's entrance, a Royal Academy member commented, "It must be exactly ten minutes before noon." He checked his watch, adjusting it slightly.

Phileas skated to the center of the room, striking a dramatic pose. "Gentlemen," he said, "today I have proven that man can break the fifty-mile-per-hour speed barrier without disrupting his internal organs!"

Before Phileas could present even a single chart to verify his accomplishment, Lord Kelvin seized the room's attention.

"Where are your qualified witnesses? Where is your Royal Academy of Science authorization?" Lord Kelvin asked, addressing Phileas. He knew Phileas had neither. "But what am I thinking? That would mean you were a *real* scientist."

The other Academy members snorted with laughter.

"By your definition, a real scientist's objective would be to *prevent* man from progress," Phileas shot back.

"We live in a golden age," Kelvin explained. "Everything worth discovering has been discovered. Yet ridiculous dreamers like you insist on a past filled with *dinosaurs* and *evolution*, and on a future filled with *motorized vehicles*, *radio waves*, and *flying machines*. All of which we *know* to be impossible!"

To the members of the Royal Academy, the exploration of these so-called fanciful ideas—ideas that would later become commonplace facts of modern existence—was a pure waste of time.

"Hear, hear!" the other academy members chanted, expressing their support of Kelvin's small-mindedness.

Phileas was about to counter their argument when Kitchner bustled into the room. "The bloody Bank of England is a madhouse!" he cried.

There was a buzz of conversation. Talk of the bank robbery seized the members' attention.

Passepartout smoothly slipped out of line, slinking toward the door.

Colonial Kitchner reassured everyone. "At this very moment, a hundred bobbies are combing the streets of London."

Passepartout abruptly backtracked, stepping back into line alongside the other valets.

"I assure you," Kitchner added, "we'll have him in the Tower of London by nightfall."

Phileas scoffed at the illogical statement.

"Twenty-six minutes ago a ship left Dover for Paris," Phileas said as he checked his pocket watch. "From there, the thief will take the Orient Express, where he will transfer to another train from Constantinople to India. In little over a month, this man could be in China!"

Passepartout brightened at Phileas's words. If true, he could be back in China in no time.

"If we're to believe Fogg's calculations," chortled Lord Salisbury, "the thief will have circled the globe and returned to England in a fortnight!"

This brought another round of laughter.

"Actually," Phileas stated matter-of-factly, "by my calculations, it would be closer to *exactly* . . . eighty days!"

Now everyone laughed. No one had ever circled the world in such a short period of time. It was impossible, they all thought.

"Outstanding idea!" Lord Kelvin teased. "Let's see *you* go around the world in eighty days."

The thought of leaving his laboratory for any length of time at all (except to conduct his experiments) was ludicrous, as far as Phileas was concerned. "That would be a fruitless use of my time," he protested softly. "I'm on the verge of countless scientific breakthroughs."

"Like those ridiculous wheelie shoes?" Kelvin snickered. The crowd joined him in fits of laughter at Phileas's expense.

"I've wasted enough time on your narrow minds!" said Phileas, deeply insulted. He headed for the door, his wheeled shoes carrying him quickly across the marble floor.

"Admit it! It cannot be done," Kelvin said, mocking Phileas.

SQUEEEAAAKK! The wheeled shoes came to an abrupt halt. Phileas turned to face Kelvin. "It can. *I* could do it. But I'd need a far better reason than proving it to *you*, Kelvin."

"There must be something I could offer you that would be worthy of your time," Kelvin pondered aloud.

"There is," Phileas said with great conviction. "Your position as head of the Royal Academy."

The room emitted a collective gasp. Then, they fell silent, stunned by the mere suggestion. One surprised member's monocle dropped from his eye, splashing into his tea.

"With the queen's ear," Phileas proclaimed, "I could lead Britain and the rest of the world into a new age of progress and discovery."

Refusing to be outdone—especially by Phileas Fogg—Lord Kelvin retorted, "I, Lord Kelvin, hereby vow to surrender my position as minister of science to Phileas Fogg, if he can circumnavigate the globe in no more than eighty days."

A second gasp filled the Royal Academy. The members were shocked. But they didn't realize the full extent of Kelvin's plan.

"However, if he can't," Lord Kelvin continued, grinning mischievously, "he must never set foot in this academy again. He must tear down that eyesore he calls a laboratory. . . ."

Always a showman, Lord Kelvin paused. Having made his audience wait before he delivered his final requirement, he concluded: "And he must swear *never to invent again!*"

Phileas trembled. Inventing was his entire life. He could never give it up. Phileas stood silently, unable to respond.

"Just as I always suspected, Fogg," Kelvin goaded. "You promise much, but you deliver nothing." Snickers rippled through the crowd.

"I'll take your wager," Phileas said meekly.

The snickering came to an abrupt halt.

"What did you say?" Lord Kelvin asked the eccentric inventor.

"I'll take your wager!" declared Phileas.

Passepartout smiled, knowing that his new employer had made a bold and courageous decision—one that would help him achieve his own goal, as well.

"Then it's done," Kelvin chuckled. "A man who has never set foot out of England will circle the globe. This is going to be rather amusing."

"History won't remember your amusement, Lord Kelvin!" Phileas said, his confidence building. "But it will be hard pressed to forget the moment I stood here, on the very steps of the Royal Academy after having traveled around the world in eighty days!"

5 ❖ IN WHICH THE JOURNEY BEGINS

PHILEAS HAD DEDICATED HIS ENTIRE LIFE to inventing. His family's fortune allowed him to devote all of his time and energy to that occupation. As Lord Kelvin mockingly pointed out, Phileas Fogg had never so much as taken a step out of England, let alone traveled around the entire world. Now, he was about to risk everything on an adventure that would take him far from the protective walls of the Fogg mansion.

As Passepartout prepared for the trip, he could tell that this prospect was unnerving his new boss. Phileas's already peculiar habits were becoming even stranger. Passepartout assumed that Phileas had not really meant to put his underwear on over his pants. And Passepartout certainly hoped that Mr. Fogg didn't have a habit of talking to his coat-rack, as he had witnessed him doing that day. When it was time to leave, Passepartout searched everywhere for his dazed and disoriented master, until he found him sitting fully dressed in an empty bathtub.

"Mr. Fogg, we're all packed and ready to go," Passepartout announced cheerfully, trying to act as though nothing were out of the ordinary.

"I'm afraid this was a calamitous lapse in judgment," Phileas said, shuddering.

Passepartout had only recently met his new employer. But Mr. Fogg seemed like a decent, honest man, whom he wanted to help. He noticed a painting on the wall, depicting Phileas with his parents. "Maybe we should let your family know," he offered.

Phileas shook his head. "There is no one left to tell. This house and my inventions are all I have."

"And a brave new French valet who will help you make it around the world in eighty days," Passepartout said encouragingly, bringing a smile to the inventor's face.

"Do you seriously believe we can succeed?" Phileas asked.

"Yes," said Passepartout, without hesitation.

"Yes! Yes!" Phileas exclaimed, with newfound enthusiasm.

He stood dramatically, and, peering down at himself, was reminded that he was still wearing his underwear on top of his pants. His doubts returned in an instant. "You're mad. We'll be sliced to pieces before we reach India!" he cried.

Outside, crowds of people had been gathering all through the morning in order to witness the beginning of Phileas Fogg's daring journey. In the past, people had merely thought of him as an eccentric loner who lived in a peculiar house. Now, he was attempting to do the impossible.

When the doors to Phileas's carriage house opened, the crowd erupted in cheers. Phileas and Passepartout rolled out in Fogg's latest invention, the horseless carriage. Future generations would recognize this vehicle as the earliest form of automobile, but, to the Londoners of the time, it was a miracle!

As the carriage pulled past the awestruck crowd, photographers snapped pictures. Phileas was thrilled.

"See, Mr. Fogg," Passepartout said, noticing

the crowd's response. "Already, people are noticing your great inventions!"

Just then, a police carriage drove up and blocked the vehicle's path, bringing it to a sudden stop. Out jumped Inspector Fix, a wiry little man with red hair and a crooked smile, which was appropriate for a crooked policeman. That morning, Fix had been hired by Lord Kelvin to prevent Phileas from winning the bet. Fix wasn't going to take any chances. He was going to stop Phileas immediately.

As he worked his way through the rowdy crowd, Fix winked at a fellow policeman. "Tell Kelvin I got him."

"Quite a contraption you've got here, Mr. Fogg," said Fix in his cockney accent.

"Thank you, Inspector," Phileas responded.

"But I'm afraid I'm going to have to detain you and your valet until further notice," Fix stated. "See, this doohickey is in violation of the city's new vehicle code."

"Vehicle code?" Phileas was shocked. How could there be a vehicle code for a vehicle just invented yesterday?

"All vehicles must be powered by horses or

other indigenous, quadruped creatures," Fix stammered, trying to make his pronouncement sound official, "excluding giraffes or any other ferocious animals deriving from the, ummm, homo specious family tree."

"That is drivel," Phileas remarked. "Now, stand aside. I am about to embark upon a journey around the world."

"Not in this monstrosity, you're not," a determined Fix replied. For emphasis, he slapped the side of the vehicle's engine, which, unfortunately for him, was extremely hot.

Passepartout instantly wrapped the reins of the carriage around Fix's shoe. He cranked the engine to life, snatching up Phileas's bags just as the carriage sped off. Fix was dragged, kicking and screaming, down the street. *CRASH!* The carriage smacked into the side of a building, burying Fix beneath it.

Phileas was stunned, but Passepartout leaped into action immediately, throwing all of their bags up onto the police carriage.

"Passepartout! Stealing a police vehicle is not an acceptable way to begin our journey," Phileas said, with conviction.

"Not stealing," Passepartout corrected. *"Borrowing."*

Phileas climbed onto the carriage and turned back to the crowd of people.

"Excuse us!" he announced. "We are just borrowing this vehicle to catch our ship to Paris."

Passepartout slapped the reins, the horses taking off with such force that Phileas fell back into his seat. The crowd cheered. The race had begun!

Hidden among the crowd were two of General Fang's Black Scorpions. They knew Passepartout's true identity, and they were determined to stop him before he could return the jade Buddha to his village in China. They plotted their next move carefully as the unlikely pair of adventurers disappeared from view.

Back at the Royal Academy, Lord Kelvin studied the entire scene through a telescope. "That idiot, Inspector Fix! What's the point in hiring a corrupt police officer if he can't even abuse the law properly?" Kelvin bellowed to the other lords. "Tell Inspector Fix to pack his bags. He's going on a little trip."

6 ◈ In Which Scorpions are Everywhere, and We Meet Monique

With its charming cafes, lush gardens, and stunning architecture, Paris—the "City of Light"—was considered by many to be the most beautiful city in the world.

Phileas Fogg couldn't have cared less. He just wanted to catch a train. And he wasn't having much luck.

"You've *lost* the Orient Express?" he stammered in total disbelief.

Phileas had planned to board that luxurious train, which ran from Paris to Constantinople. It was the fastest way to get from Europe to Asia.

"How does one lose an entire train?" Phileas demanded.

The clerk smirked rather than answering.

Phileas wondered if perhaps this were some new form of French communication.

"Sir, do you speak English?" Phileas asked, nearing his wits' end.

"Oui," said the clerk, and abruptly he turned his back on Phileas.

Phileas whirled to face Passepartout, who was struggling with their luggage. "Passepartout, will you tell this impudent fellow we *must* leave within six and one half hours, or we will miss our connection in Constantinople!"

"Yes, sir," replied Passepartout. He stepped up to the clerk. "Please, we are in a great hurry," he pleaded, in English (because, of course, he had no idea how to speak French).

"Passepartout!" exclaimed Phileas. "Speak in French!"

Realizing that he'd have to bluff in order to continue his charade, Passepartout let forth a mouthful of gibberish that he hoped sounded like French. Many of the words he used he merely made up, his tongue moving in odd and unusual ways to create them.

"Imbecile! You do not speak a word of French!" the clerk scoffed in his native tongue. Passepartout nodded, pretending to understand.

It was then that Passepartout noticed the two Chinese men sitting at a nearby café, being served by a Chinese waiter—an unusual sight in Paris. Further along the block, another Chinese man pushed a fruit cart. Near that, yet another Chinese man painted a caricature. None of the men seemed to be paying attention to what they were doing. They all seemed to be watching Passepartout.

Passepartout realized that these must be the Black Scorpions—sent by General Fang to steal back the jade Buddha.

"The next train will leave in five hours," Passepartout announced, pulling on Phileas's sleeve, determined to get him out of any possible danger. "It's a good time for sightseeing!"

"This is a scientific expedition, not a holiday!" an exasperated Phileas replied. "I will not chance missing the train."

The Black Scorpions headed toward them.

Knowing he needed to get Phileas away before the deadly men attacked, Passepartout searched for an excuse. The poster of a giant lightbulb proved to be the inspiration he needed.

"Look! Very amazing," he said, pretending to read the French writing on the poster.

"What does it say?" Phileas inquired.

Moving his finger along the poster's words—hoping it would convince Phileas, Passepartout claimed that the American inventor Thomas Edison was in Paris, exhibiting his latest inventions.

The chance to meet the great Edison was too much for Phileas to pass up. After all, Edison was one of Phileas's heroes.

Passepartout hustled a now-willing Phileas out of the train station just as the Black Scorpions closed in.

Passepartout realized he was being chased once again. Now, however, he was trying to hide from the dangerous Black Scorpions. He also had to keep Phileas safe while keeping him moving, all without raising his suspicions.

Desperate for a place to hide, Passepartout spotted the entrance to a nearby gallery. Claiming that the sign outside advertised a scientific exhibition, Passepartout was able to slip Phileas indoors just before the Black Scorpions arrived.

Inside the crowded gallery, it didn't take long for Phileas to realize there was no "scientific exhibition." The walls were covered with bright, colorful paintings.

"Wait a moment," Phileas exclaimed. "This is not science! This is *art*!" He practically spat out the word.

Making his way through the gallery, he scoffed at the works. "That painting is highly inaccurate."

His statement caught the attention of a woman standing beside him and his assistant. She was young, beautiful, and more than a little upset.

"It isn't supposed to be accurate," she explained. "The artist views reality through imagination, rather than simply recording it. It's called *Impressionism*."

"Well, I am not *impressed*," Phileas stated, pleased with his play on words. "Trees are not violet. Grass is not chartreuse. And a man cannot . . ."

He stopped, drawn to the painting before him. In it, a man soared through the air. The painting was highly similar to Phileas's dreams (minus that annoying chicken).

". . . Fly," Phileas finished, his words faint and without conviction.

"Do you dream of flying?" she asked.

"Sometimes," he answered, captivated. The painting was his lifelong dream realized, even if it was only in canvas and paint. One day, Phileas knew, it would be reality.

"I'm glad you like my painting," the woman said. She introduced herself: "I am Monique Larouche."

"Phileas Fogg," he returned, still fascinated by the picture. "I must say, it's an awful lot better than these amateurs'."

"What did he say?" asked a one-eared man standing nearby. Phileas ignored the man, having no idea that the latter would be famous throughout history as Vincent van Gogh, one of the greatest artists of all time. Van Gogh returned his focus to his painting—one he had titled *Starry Night*—and put the finishing touches on it. Neither of them knew it would one day be considered his masterpiece.

To Phileas, the only picture in the room that was worthy of a second look was Monique's portrait of the man in flight.

The gallery manager, however, disagreed. He walked up to Monique scowling.

"Who is responsible for this vandalism?" he

asked, in French, indicating Monique's picture.

"It is mine," Monique proudly stated. "Does it please you?"

"No!" responded the manager. "You want to hang something? Get back in the closet and hang people's coats, as you were hired to do. In fact, don't," he continued. "You're fired. Leave art to the artists!"

The manager yanked Monique's painting from the wall and shoved it at her.

Because the argument had been conducted in French, Phileas was more than a little confused. "What was that all about?" he asked Monique.

Devastated, Monique tried to cover her embarrassment. "A wealthy gentleman bought my painting for a lot of money," she lied, forcing a brave smile. "Champagne for everyone!"

Looking outside, Passepartout noticed the three Black Scorpions passing by the window. Before he could get out of the way, the last of General Fang's agents spotted him.

Passepartout quickly scanned the room, but there was no means of escape. He was going to have to fight the Black Scorpions right there in the gallery.

7 ❖ IN WHICH THE JOURNEY RESUMES, DESPITE MANY OBSTACLES

As THE THREE BLACK SCORPIONS ENTERED the gallery, Passepartout rushed up the stairs, leaped out of the second-story window, and finally slipped back inside the building again, through another window. If it worked with bobbies, Passepartout thought, it might work with the Black Scorpions.

Meanwhile, Phileas continued his conversation with Monique, blissfully unaware of Passepartout's predicament.

"Have you ever considered a career in schematic drawing?" Phileas asked the pretty artist.

"Like what an engineer does?" she asked. "No. It would be far too limiting."

"Limiting?" Phileas scoffed. "Science is the only way to explore the depth of man's knowledge."

Monique stuck to her point. "Art is the only way to explore the depth of a man's soul! Art reminds us our imagination is limitless."

Passepartout, still pursued by the Black Scorpions, dashed about the gallery. "Don't worry, Mr. Fogg. These men are going to help me find Mr. Edison," Passepartout fibbed cleverly, so as not to have to explain why ruthless killers were chasing him.

"This way!" he gestured, waving to the Black Scorpions as he sprinted out of the room, the lethal agents still on his tail.

"He's very eager," commented Phileas.

Monique handed him her most prized possession—her sketchbook. "I haven't felt very inspired lately," she warned him.

Phileas flipped through her sketches—angry clowns, dogs playing poker—not his cup of tea.

"I'm a scientist. Perhaps I'm not the best judge," Phileas said politely, closing the sketchbook.

Meanwhile, Passepartout found himself cornered

in the back studio of the gallery, surrounded by several frightening Black Scorpions and a room full of empty canvases and paint. A fight erupted. Passepartout, defending himself from his attackers with anything he could grab—paintbrushes, canvases, easels, even the paint itself—turned the studio into a flurry of flying colors as blank canvases were splattered with paint.

Passepartout, now covered in paint, hurled an easel directly at the Black Scorpions and dashed back into the main gallery.

"Bandits!" he screamed, addressing the gallery patrons, including Phileas and Monique. "They've come to take away all the paintings!"

Monique signaled to Phileas and Passepartout. "Quickly," she said. "In there!" She grabbed her bag of painting supplies and pushed against one of the murals. It swung on hinges to reveal a secret room behind it. They rushed into the room and hid themselves for the moment from the Black Scorpions.

Then Monique led them out of the secret room, down an underground tunnel, and up through a trapdoor in the ceiling. They emerged aboveground in the middle of the Tuileries, an enchanting public garden.

"Thank you, Miss Larouche," said Phileas. "You may just have saved our trip around the world. I would really like to repay you—"

"You are going on a trip?" said Monique, fascinated. "Take me with you!"

Phileas was shocked. "I beg your pardon?"

"I am stifled here," said Monique. "Pigeonholed. They think of me only as . . . a coat-check girl."

"Why?" said Phileas.

"Because . . . I *am* the coat-check girl," Monique admitted, meekly. "I need a world journey to inspire me."

Just then, the three Black Scorpions appeared across the park, charging straight toward them. Passepartout scanned the scene for an escape route and discovered the perfect getaway—a hot-air balloon!

"I am inspired to get us back on schedule," Passepartout said confidently as he pointed toward the balloon. Phileas, always the scientist, pulled out his multipurpose travel cane and pressed a few buttons. Out popped a weather vane and a compass.

"Let's see," Phileas said, examining the data.

"Current temperature, sixty-three degrees. Wind velocity, approximately twelve knots. Factoring in the hot air density . . ." Phileas calculated the results in his head. "Outstanding, Passepartout! Onward!"

The three dashed over to the balloon, cutting in front of the long line of people waiting to take a ride in it.

"Keep the change," Phileas said as he tossed the balloonist a large wad of cash.

Phileas and Passepartout climbed into the basket, but Monique was not about to let them get away.

"We are going around the world!" she stated excitedly as she climbed aboard with them.

Phileas was dismayed. "The balloon cannot support all this weight," he said.

"Your hot air will compensate," she shot back.

Passepartout untied the mooring ropes, and the balloon began its ascent. Phileas felt around for his valise, then gasped in horror. He looked down at the line of angry people and saw a crazy old woman holding the valise.

"Passepartout," he cried out. "My valise! It has all my money in it!"

The devoted valet jumped out of the basket and slid down the mooring ropes, landing in front of the old Frenchwoman. He grabbed the valise, but she refused to let go.

"It's not your bag," he shouted. "It's our bag."

"No, it's my bag!" she retorted, and proceeded to bite him on the arm, though she had no teeth.

Passepartout giggled instead of screaming.

"Hey, that tickles!" he remarked as he tossed the valise back up to his employer.

Passepartout leaped for the drifting mooring rope, only to find that the Black Scorpions had closed in around him. He valiantly battled them with a flurry of kicks and punches. Onlookers scattered, to avoid the skirmish.

Just as the balloon got nearly out of reach, Passepartout grabbed the mooring rope, a moment before the balloon floated upward, out of the Black Scorpions' grasp.

"We almost lost your valet," Monique remarked to Phileas.

"It wouldn't be the first time," he replied.

The Black Scorpions continued to chase Passepartout as he dangled helplessly from the balloon. He slammed into everything in the balloon's path—buildings, walls, street vendors.

Phileas frantically tried to master the controls. "We must save Passepartout!" he exclaimed. "How do I make this go lower?"

Monique grabbed a sandbag from the side of the balloon and dangled it over the edge.

"What are you doing?" he asked her, exasperated. "If you *decrease* the weight, it won't work."

"Yes, it will," she said with a wry smile, dropping the sandbag straight on top of a Black Scorpion's head, knocking him out cold.

"Physics, no?" she asked coyly.

"Yes," Phileas smiled, impressed.

Passepartout held on tightly to the end of the rope as the balloon sailed across the Paris skyline.

Phileas was relieved. Passepartout was now safe, and despite the unexpected detour, they would float to Munich, catch up with the Orient Express, and get back on schedule.

As for Monique, Phileas was determined that she would return to Paris. Monique, however, had a much different plan.

8 ◈ IN WHICH THE PROBLEM OF SPEED IS ADDRESSED

ALREADY WORRIED about running into any more delays, Phileas found it frustrating that Monique was still traveling with them when they boarded the Orient Express in Munich. The elegant train's route, from Paris to Constantinople, Turkey, snaked through the Alps, with a view of some of the most picturesque landscapes in the world.

Monique happily sketched one such landscape. "Look at that sunrise," she marveled, trying to capture on paper the explosion of colored light. "There's only one word for it—magical!"

"There's another word for it," Phileas replied drily. "Refraction." He explained: "As the sun emerges from the horizon, we see it through more layers of atmosphere than before, making it appear more colorful. Hardly magical."

"Do you always reduce everything to a scientific formula?" Monique asked, smiling.

Passepartout couldn't help answering for Phileas. "Sometimes he makes a graph."

Monique and Passepartout shared a chuckle. But Phileas was in no mood for joking.

"Miss Larouche, I have tried to be a gentleman. But I refuse to allow you to continue traveling with us," he said firmly.

"I am not traveling with you," she retorted. "I'm making my own way. Maybe *you* shouldn't travel with *me*."

The double-talk frustrated Phileas even more. "This is what happens when you leave your home," he said grouchily. "You meet . . . people!" He stomped toward the front of the train.

With Phileas gone, Monique leaned in and confronted Passepartout.

"You are as French as a plate of spaghetti!" she exclaimed. "What are you trying to hide?"

Passepartout did not want to reveal his secret, but realized he had no choice. She was onto him.

"A sacred object was stolen from my village in China," he explained. "I have to bring it back."

Passepartout removed the beautiful jade Buddha from his leather pouch, revealing it to the stunned Monique. The Buddha sparkled majestically in the early morning light.

"For many centuries, the jade Buddha has protected my people," said Passepartout. "It never left our village . . . until now." He explained that the statue had been stolen by General Fang, with the help of the Black Scorpions, so that she could take over Passepartout's village.

"I must return the jade Buddha, to protect Lanzhou," he said. "Traveling with Mr. Fogg is the fastest way."

"Maybe we can help one another," bargained Monique. "I will keep your secret if you convince Mr. Fogg to let me travel the world with you."

Before he could respond, Phileas returned, escorted roughly back to his seat by two angry German trainmen.

The engineer warned Phileas that if he interfered with their work again, he would be thrown off the train. Then the trainmen stormed back to the locomotive.

"I merely pointed out that if they coordinated their coal-shoveling technique, they would maximize their speed," Phileas explained.

Picking up where he had left off earlier, Phileas remarked to Monique: "When we arrive in Constantinople, I suggest you board a train that *we* are not on."

Monique protested, but Phileas would not bend. "Soon our path turns dangerous," he said. "India, the Middle East. Not suitable places for a woman."

"Monsieur Fogg, if *I* can make the train go faster, may I come with you?" she proposed.

Phileas considered her idea, then nodded—confident that she could do no such thing.

"I bid you farewell, Miss Larouche," Phileas said, as she headed for the engine car.

Phileas was stunned when, moments later, the train began to pick up speed.

Monique reentered the passenger car, escorted by the trainmen who had scolded Phileas earlier. They were now in a very pleasant mood.

"If there is anything else you would like," the engineer said, "please just let us know, Miss Larouche."

"You are both so kind," Monique said, batting her eyelashes. Retaking her seat, she turned to Phileas. "Can science explain *that*?"

Phileas scowled.

Monique then used her persuasive charm to have the three of them moved to the first-class section of the train. There they dined on delicious food, drank champagne, and relaxed on comfortable, velvet seats.

Continuing his charade as a valet, Passepartout obeyed Phileas's precise schedule, and at 4:13 P.M. he headed off to make his employer's tea. Left alone, Phileas had no idea what to say to Monique. He had spent his entire life among inventions. He was totally lost around people—especially people as enchanting as Monique.

Back in the serving car, Passepartout used a thermometer to ensure that the tea was at the precise temperature Phileas demanded. Unused to the chores of a valet, Passepartout bumped into the kettle, spilling hot water onto the leather pouch. He quickly removed the jade Buddha to make sure it was unharmed.

The door suddenly opened. Inspector Fix, searching the train for Phileas, stood outside. At

banquet tonight," the soldier announced.

Monique seemed thrilled with the offer, but Phileas declared himself not interested. "How very flattering," he replied. "But please inform Prince Hapi that we are on a very tight schedule."

"This train will not move until you do so," the soldier answered curtly.

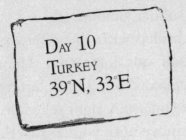

DAY 10
TURKEY
39°N, 33°E

9 ❖ IN WHICH THE TRAVELERS MEET HAPI

TURKEY, THE GATEWAY TO ASIA, featured beautiful architecture that combined ancient and modern styles. Colorful mosaic tiles decorated many buildings.

To Phileas, there simply was no time to appreciate any of it. And, certainly, there was no time to visit royalty. But he had no choice.

Riding in the prince's royal carriage, the trio were stunned by the sight of the giant palace that awaited them. "It is magnificent!" Monique exclaimed.

Passepartout was impressed, too. "Mr. Fogg, his house is even bigger than yours," he joked.

Phileas shot him a dirty look. "Perhaps the

prince is looking for a new valet," he said.

Inside the palace, they discovered a lavish party in progress. Young women wearing silken veils danced to music played by a dashing, muscle-bound guitar player.

"Where is His Highness?" Monique asked one of the soldiers, expecting to find Prince Hapi sitting on a jeweled throne. Much to her surprise, the soldier pointed to the guitar player himself.

"That man is Prince Hapi?" she said, very impressed.

"I suppose if I did nothing but lounge about the palace all day, I would learn to pluck a few notes," Phileas muttered jealously.

Prince Hapi finished his musical performance with an elaborate guitar solo, stunning all who witnessed it. The crowd around the prince burst into applause as Phileas seethed.

"Ah! My guests have arrived," Prince Hapi exclaimed as he set down his guitar.

"All right, we'll make this brief," Phileas said in an aside to Passepartout. "I will pose for a few photographs, perhaps wearing a turban and holding an atlas."

Prince Hapi could not have cared less about

Phileas. His eyes were immediately drawn to the beautiful Monique. "Mademoiselle, how magical that our paths should cross," he said as he kissed her hand. "Do you believe in fate?"

He looked deeply into her eyes. Monique couldn't help blushing.

"Is it fate when a person stops a moving train and kidnaps its passengers?" Phileas retorted.

"Phileas Fogg, please forgive me," Hapi said, still gazing at Monique. "But I feel as though Aphrodite herself had descended to earth!"

Phileas stepped away, unimpressed with Hapi's foolish, romantic gestures. His eyes wandered to a particularly interesting statue of a crouching man, with tremendous, rippling muscles. Phileas pointed at it. "Is that a—"

"No! Don't touch it!" Hapi screamed. "That is my most treasured possession."

Monique thought it an exquisite work of art.

"Is that a—" she began.

"Yes, a Rodin." Hapi beamed with pride. Auguste Rodin was a famous French sculptor. For Prince Hapi personally to own one of Rodin's works was very impressive.

But that was not nearly as impressive as

Monique's discovery that the statue was of Prince Hapi himself! Those were *his* bulging muscles.

"Incredible," Monique gasped. "It is a sculpture of you?"

"Yes," Hapi replied, almost sheepishly. "I am in much better shape now. Come, we must dine!"

Later, after feasting on a huge dinner, Prince Hapi and the travelers relaxed in a big, warm swimming pool.

The prince slid his arm around Monique slyly, enamored of her charm and beauty.

Phileas seethed.

"Miss Larouche," said the prince, as he offered her a plump strawberry. "It is mesmerizing to watch the way your face illuminates when your senses are aroused."

Monique took a bite of the strawberry and smiled nervously.

Typically, Phileas offered a scientific explanation. "Her discoloration could be easily interpreted as an allergic reaction. Or perhaps even a mild form of hives."

Prince Hapi and Monique laughed giddily.

"Although, I have noticed," Phileas observed, "that there is a certain luminous glow in her complexion when she's drawing."

Phileas's words surprised even him. Did he feel more for Monique than he realized?

Monique was touched. For the first time, she realized that Phileas might have had special feelings for her, too.

"We should be going," she said politely. "Thank you for your hospitality, Prince Hapi."

The prince was displeased. "The gentlemen are free to go," he announced. "But Miss Larouche stays here . . . to become my wife."

Monique gasped.

"Wife number seven," Prince Hapi added.

"You have seven wives!" she exclaimed, appalled.

"One for each day of the week," he said, with a sly smile. "Do Tuesdays work for you?"

Phileas and Passepartout insisted that Monique depart with them, but Prince Hapi's soldiers approached and drew their swords. The unwanted duo gathered their belongings, waved, and headed for the palace exit.

They had no intention, however, of leaving Monique behind. They were merely devising a plan of escape. As they passed the priceless statue of Prince Hapi, they grabbed it, pushing it till it stood precariously near the edge of its pedestal.

"Halt, or Hapi gets smashed!" said Phileas forcefully.

"Anything but my statue of me!" Hapi begged.

The soldiers froze in their tracks, unsure of what to do.

With the statue as a hostage, Phileas issued his demands. "All of you, into the back room! You too, Prince! Monique comes with us!"

"Do as he says!" Prince Hapi ordered, keeping a nervous eye on his beloved statue. He reluctantly led his soldiers into the back room, where they could not see the guests escaping.

Monique gladly rejoined Phileas and Passepartout, more than ready to leave Prince Hapi and the palace behind. A nervous Phileas started to lose his grip on the statue, which he and Passepartout had been holding on to the whole time. Passepartout strengthened his hold, but it was too late. The statue slipped from their grasp and smashed into a thousand pieces.

"Get them!" Hapi screamed, enraged. The soldiers rushed the adventurers, swords drawn.

The trio dashed outside the palace doors,

Phileas still held on to a muscular arm that had broken off the statue.

"The arm!" Passepartout cried.

Phileas had an idea. He wedged the stone arm between the handles of the palace doors to bar the way against the soldiers.

Monique smiled at Phileas as they rushed away from the palace.

"Thank you," she said. "That was very heroic."

"Yes," stammered Phileas. "And needlessly time-consuming. This is exactly why I should never have let you come along. . . ."

Monique smiled and gently kissed Phileas on the cheek, rendering him speechless.

It's hard to argue with such an enchanting woman, he thought.

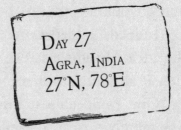

Day 27
Agra, India
27°N, 78°E

10 ❖ In Which an Escape by Elephant Nearly Succeeds

Lord Kelvin was already distraught, because Phileas had not yet been stopped. The telegram he received in his London office made him even more upset.

After recovering from his fight aboard the Orient Express, Inspector Fix had sent word that Passepartout was actually the bank robber—and had possession of Kelvin's prized jade Buddha.

"That numskull Fogg doesn't even realize he's transporting the bank thief!" Kelvin complained to his usual assortment of lords.

"Or does he?" Lord Salisbury conjectured, hatching a plan. "He did leave town in quite a hurry, wouldn't you say, Lord Rhodes?"

"Indeed," added Lord Rhodes, latching on to the idea. "Evading arrest, stealing a police vehicle—it all sounds rather incriminating to me."

"One could almost infer that this entire bet was merely a ruse to facilitate his escape," Lord Salisbury concluded.

Lord Kelvin was thrilled by the idea of accusing Phileas of masterminding the bank robbery. "Brilliant, Lord Salisbury! I shall name a beef-related entrée after you in your honor," he said.

Salisbury was pleased.

Kelvin turned to Colonel Kitchner. "Inform your men at Scotland Yard that Phileas Fogg is without a doubt the man who robbed the Bank of England!"

Luckily for Kelvin, the travelers were crossing India, a British territory.

"I want their faces posted in every police station, army barracks, post office, railway station, and outhouse in India," he thundered. "We're going to stop Fogg and get my jade Buddha back by any means necessary!"

After examining maps of the region, it was decided that the best place to capture Phileas was in the ancient city of Agra. Agra was known as the home of the Taj Mahal, a building that was considered one of the most beautiful in the world. Now, it might also become known as the place where Phileas Fogg's journey around the world came to an abrupt end.

Riding the train from Bombay to Calcutta, Phileas tabulated every moment of their journey. Each calculation led to the same conclusion: it would be a race to the finish, with no time to spare.

Nearby, a group of Indian children surrounded Passepartout, listening eagerly as he told them the legend of the Ten Tigers of Canton—the greatest kung fu fighters in history.

"They fought to keep order and justice in China," he told them.

"Did they really fight like tigers?" asked a boy.

"Yes," Passepartout answered. "Each Tiger had his own 'animal' fighting style." Passepartout acted out the different animal styles as he explained: "The crane, the snake, the monkey . . ."

"The goat!" Phileas cried, swatting at the animal in question, which was currently nibbling on his pages of calculations. The goat was just one of many animals riding in the train car with them.

"Passepartout, stop this filthy animal!" Phileas complained. "And refrain from your ridiculous anecdotes," he sternly commanded.

"Why do you not like his story, Mr. Frog?" one of the boys asked, mispronouncing Phileas's name.

"Because the story is implausible," Phileas answered. "How can a man learn to defend himself by watching animals behave like . . . animals?"

In Phileas's mind, all great lessons began with human beings and their studies of science.

"But it's a famous legend," Monique protested.

"It is a ridiculous legend," Phileas answered.

"Most legends are born from truth," said an Indian girl.

"Yes, but all truths are born from facts," said Phileas. "Facts that can be written down on paper."

"And then eaten by a goat?" asked Monique wryly. She and the children laughed. Phileas was *not* amused.

Metal screeched as the train came to a sudden stop. Phileas groaned. "Not another delay!"

Passepartout peered out the window. The area was swarming with British soldiers—many of them carrying copies of a Wanted poster of Phileas and Passepartout.

Once again, Passepartout found himself on the run. "Time to go," he barked, scrambling to collect his little group's luggage.

"What is the meaning of this?" Phileas demanded.

Passepartout cringed. He had to tell Phileas the truth—or at least some of it. "They seem to think we robbed the Bank of England."

"That's preposterous," Phileas scoffed. "This is merely a desperate attempt by Lord Kelvin to impede my journey. I am a British citizen, and I have nothing to fear!"

Gunshots erupted outside, startling everyone on the train.

Especially Phileas.

". . . Except bullets," Phileas admitted fearfully.

The trio tried to flee the train, but found their way blocked by British soldiers, posters in hand. Passepartout scanned for a means of escape—and found one, in the form of an elephant.

Elephants were common in India. They were also very large: large enough, in fact, to hide three adults who were at that moment considered fugitives by the British soldiers.

A small group of soldiers gathered near the

train, confused at not having found the bank robbers on board. The soldiers took no notice of the elephant that lumbered past them.

On the other side of the giant animal, the fugitives clung to the guide's seat.

The plan seemed foolproof. They would ride the elephant just clear of the British soldiers and then out of Agra. Pleased with their ingenious escape plan, Passepartout gave the elephant an encouraging pat on the side.

The elephant misunderstood the pat as a signal and slowly began to turn—in the direction of the British soldiers!

"Bad elephant!" Passepartout whispered, trying in vain to get the animal to stop. It was no use. The elephant continued to turn, completely exposing the trio to the soldiers' view.

The trio jumped down and hurried off, slipping into the crowd. Nearby, Passepartout noticed three Indian women selling olives—giving him another idea.

After a brief period of haggling, the three adventurers were able to walk right past the soldiers, the newly-bought Indian clothing in which they were dressed (complete with veils to hide their faces) perfectly disguising them as women.

None of the soldiers gave the three "women" a second glance.

"Stay calm," Passepartout whispered as they passed the soldiers. "Just act like ladies."

"Not a problem," Monique assured him.

"I feel faint," Phileas said, overdramatically.

"Women are not that frail," Monique said defensively.

"No," Phileas countered. "But, I am."

Phileas wasn't sure whether he was about to faint or be sick. Once the three had passed the soldiers, he made a beeline for the nearest out-house. He reached the door just as it swung open, and found himself face to face with its current occupant—Inspector Fix.

11 ❖ IN WHICH
FAMILIAR ENEMIES ARE
EVERYWHERE

PHILEAS FROZE at the sight of the crooked policeman. But Fix didn't recognize Phileas. To the
inspector, Phileas just looked like an ordinary
Indian woman, albeit a very strange-looking one.

"Hello darlin'," Fix said with a flash of charm.
"What can I do for you?"

"Maulll. . . . yeeeeaaaa. . . . mahllllyeaaa,"
Phileas babbled, trying his hardest to sound as
though he were speaking Hindi. Phileas slammed
the outhouse door, smacking it right into Fix's
already broken nose. The inspector yelped in pain
and bumped his head on the back of the out-
house, knocking himself out cold.

Panicked, Phileas ran back to Passepartout and Monique. Just as he had warned them he might, he fainted right into Passepartout's arms.

Things were not going well. Passepartout signaled the driver of a *palki gharry*, a two-wheeled cart pulled by a man instead of a horse.

Passepartout and Monique hurriedly climbed onto the vehicle, helping Phileas, who was still passed out.

"Get us out of Agra, quickly!" Passepartout ordered. The driver nodded and started pulling the cart.

"We did it!" sighed Monique.

They were so relieved to be heading away from danger that neither of them noticed the black scorpion tattooed on the driver's forearm.

The driver abruptly turned the *palki gharry* down a dead-end alley and threw Passepartout right out of the cart.

The driver ripped off his Indian *palki gharry* driver disguise, revealing a hulking body—even more muscular than Prince Hapi's—with thick chains that crossed his chest. He was a Black Scorpion!

"Phileas! Passepartout!" gasped Monique.

The Black Scorpion flashed a menacing smile. With his bare hands, he bent the metal fender of the *palki gharry* around Monique's wrist, pinning her to the cart.

Passepartout gathered his bearings and stood up, readying himself for another battle, when suddenly he heard a familiar voice.

"Fogg's valet! Now I gotcha!" Smiling proudly, Inspector Fix slapped a pair of handcuffs on Passepartout's wrist, clamping the valet to himself.

The Black Scorpion didn't care who was chained to whom; he swung a spiked mace, aiming for Fix and Passepartout.

Passepartout grabbed Fix and pushed him to the ground, throwing himself down, too, to avoid the swirling mass of steel.

"Run!" Passepartout shouted, but he and Fix fled in opposite directions, the handcuffs pulling tightly, snapping them both back to the point where they had started.

The Black Scorpion continued his attack. Passepartout cleverly used Fix as a shield—spinning him in the direction of incoming punches.

Being dragged by the horseless carriage and falling off the Orient Express were love taps compared to the beating Fix was now receiving.

"Who is this man? What's upsetting him?" Fix cried out, between the bone-crushing blows.

"He wants the jade Buddha, too!" Passepartout answered, yanking Fix upstairs toward a balcony.

"Then, give it to him!" Fix wailed in desperation.

Meanwhile, Monique had freed herself from the *palki gharry* and was trying to escape. There was only one problem.

"Wake up!" she yelled at the dazed Phileas, shaking him.

A female Black Scorpion agent sprang from a nearby rooftop, landing perfectly at the mouth of the alley. She stalked toward Monique, whipping a sharp sword back and forth.

Monique crouched into what she hoped was a dramatic kung fu pose, trying to fake her way out of the situation. The female Black Scorpion was not impressed. She grabbed Monique and effortlessly lifted her off the ground, hanging her on a nearby hook. Monique squirmed, unable to free herself, and the Black Scorpion prepared to finish her off.

"Phileas! Help!" she cried, finally rousing him to consciousness.

"I had a terrible dream," Phileas said, still a bit bleary. "I turned into an Indian woman." He looked down and realized that his reality wasn't far from what his dream had foretold.

Then, he snapped into action, stumbling out of the *palki gharry* and landing awkwardly on his back on the ground.

"I'll protect you," he proclaimed, grabbing his cane and leaping in between Monique and the female Black Scorpion.

"This cane is not as it appears," Phileas bragged, tossing it from hand to hand. "If I depress this button, it will deploy a weapon far more deadly than yours."

He pressed the button, and out popped a sextant, an ancient navigational tool. It was a handy instrument, but hardly a threat.

"This . . ." Phileas bluffed, "is a . . . strange knife."

"Isn't it a sextant?" said the Black Scorpion.

"Yes," Phileas feebly admitted.

He twirled his cane, his finger accidentally hitting another button. An umbrella shot right out of the top of the cane, dislodging a canopy from a nearby fruit cart. The canopy swung down,

Phileas Fogg considers his travel plans. Can he make it around the world in just 80 days?

Passepartout is happy to be Phileas's new valet—and to get to China quickly!

The stolen jade Buddha! Now Passepartout must return the prized possession to his village.

Inspector Fix wants to put a stop to Phileas's travel plans.

The journey begins with a stylish ride.

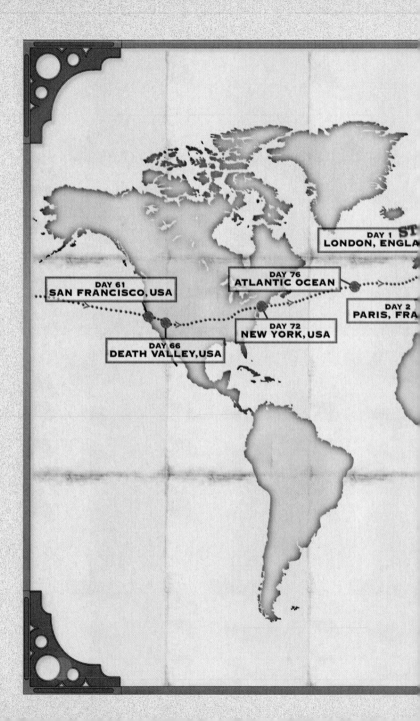

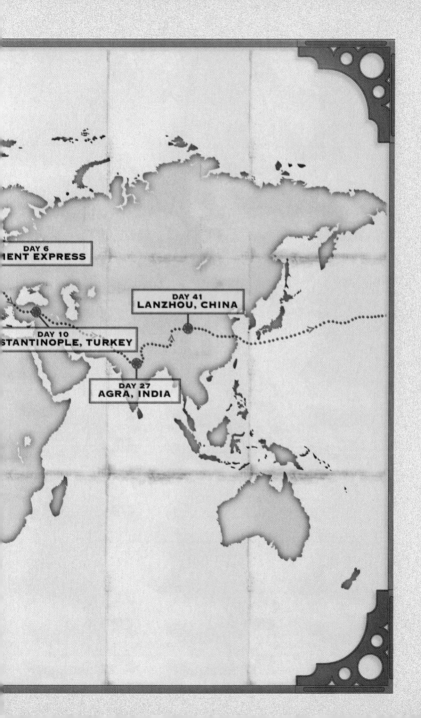

DAY 6
ENT EXPRESS

DAY 41
LANZHOU, CHINA

DAY 10
STANTINOPLE, TURKEY

DAY 27
AGRA, INDIA

Monique and Phileas escape the Black Scorpions by jumping into a hot-air balloon.

Phileas and Passepartout come across some pretty shocking sights during their travels.

After a narrow escape and a paint fight, Passepartout gets a lift.

A jet pack can get you there fast!

Away they go on Phileas's new invention—the flying machine.

Queen Victoria is a big fan of Phileas Fogg. She wants him to win his wager!

smacking the female Black Scorpion in the back of the head and knocking her out cold.

Phileas turned to Monique, feeling brave and heroic. He unhooked her and she fell right into his arms.

"Phileas," she breathed. "That was so unlike you."

Gazing at her, Phileas leaned in for a kiss.

"We should run," Monique said.

"Yes, we should," Phileas sadly agreed.

They dashed back to the center of the market-place, where Passepartout had knocked out both the giant Black Scorpion and Inspector Fix.

They had fended off Fang's agents and Kelvin's corrupt policeman, but they were still stuck in Agra, where British soldiers were on the lookout for Phileas.

"Oh, dear!" Phileas whispered, as he saw a group of soldiers approaching. "The worst person in the world to be right now is me!"

That gave Passepartout a wonderful idea. He quickly dressed Inspector Fix in some of Fogg's clothes and laid him in the back of the *palki gharry*, pushing it into the crowd.

"It is him," Monique shouted, in her best attempt at an Indian accent. "The Englishman who robbed the Bank of England. He's trying to escape!"

From behind, rolling through the crowd in a *palki gharry*, Inspector Fix looked exactly like Fogg. The British soldiers charged right past Phileas and Passepartout, converging on the unwitting policeman.

"Let's go!" Passepartout cried.

Phileas scanned his maps, trying to find the quickest escape route. Most of the usual travel routes across Asia led through British territories, where there would be even more soldiers looking for them.

"Does England own everything in Asia?" asked a frustrated Monique.

Passepartout smiled. "Not China," he said with pride. "Not yet!"

Phileas nodded. It was agreed. They would head for China.

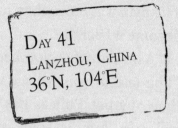

DAY 41
LANZHOU, CHINA
36°N, 104°E

12 ❖ IN WHICH
LAU XING GOES HOME

THE MOUNTAIN PASS THAT LED INTO CHINA was filled with lush greenery and a sparkling river that wound its way alongside the path.

Passepartout steered the ox-drawn cart down the path; his traveling companions were asleep in the back of the transport. Though he was relieved to be back in his native land, even the calming flow of the river couldn't quell his unease.

"You look troubled," said Monique.

Passepartout nodded. After checking to make sure that Phileas was still asleep, he answered her. "I cannot keep lying to Mr. Fogg," he said, keeping his voice low.

He felt guilty for taking advantage of Phileas.

The man was more than just his employer. He had become a friend.

"You did what you had to," Monique offered. "The fate of your village is of far greater concern than any bet Phileas has made. If he loses, all it will cost him is some money and pride. Two things he has plenty of anyway."

Passepartout was about to explain that Phileas would also have to close his laboratory and stop inventing. But then something wonderful caught his eye.

"My village!" he beamed as Lanzhou came into view. The village was a collection of thatched-roof huts and farmlands, seated at the base of a lush mountain.

"Your village?" said Phileas, waking up confused.

"I meant, 'My, what a village!'" Passepartout said, covering his mistake.

Within moments, the villagers had arrived to greet them. News spread quickly that Passepartout had returned—with the precious jade Buddha in hand! He received a hero's welcome. A group of children surrounded him, chanting his real name. "Lau Xing! Lau Xing!"

Phileas couldn't understand why they were so happy to see his valet. "Goodness, that's quite a welcome," he said to Monique. "Do these people know him?"

"It must be their custom," she answered, hoping to aid Passepartout in his ruse. "The way they welcome all strangers."

That night, the entire village celebrated in honor of the safe return of their sacred jade Buddha and the heroic Lau Xing.

The villagers offered their guests endless amounts of food and wine. Exhausted and woozy, Phileas finally staggered into a bedroom and collapsed onto one of the beds.

He was just about to drift off to sleep when something caught his eye. A series of photographs lined a nearby desktop. Many of the images showed Passepartout.

Phileas sat up, his exhaustion lifting. He studied the photos more closely. One photograph was unmistakably a family portrait.

Beside the photo sat the telegram Passepartout had sent from London. Phileas picked it up, reading it aloud. "Dear Father, I have taken back what was stolen from us. . . ."

Phileas was stunned.

The laughter in the dining room came to an

abrupt halt as Phileas stormed back in, clutching the telegram in his hand.

Passepartout rose to his feet. "Mr. Fogg, I was going to tell you—"

Phileas stopped him. "This is your family."

Passepartout did not deny it. Instead, he told Phileas what he had wanted to tell him for a long time. "My name is not Passepartout. It is Lau Xing. I robbed the Bank of England."

"*You* robbed the Bank of England?" Phileas echoed in disbelief.

"Not for gold or money, but for the jade Buddha," Passepartout explained. "It was stolen from our village."

"He had no other choice," Monique said. "This was his only way to get home."

"*You* knew about this?" questioned Phileas, realizing that Monique had betrayed him, as well. Anger swelled inside him.

"I have nothing but respect for you, Mr. Fogg," pleaded Passepartout.

"Then respect my deductive reasoning," said Phileas. "You both used me. You to escape to China!" he said, glaring at Passepartout. To Monique, he cried, "And you, to travel the world to further your Impressionistic humbug!"

He was heartbroken. "Your overtures of comradeship or friendship . . . all of it was a means to ensure that I would take you both along."

Passepartout and Monique sat speechless. They really were his friends, but they knew that no matter what they said now, he wouldn't believe them. Phileas snatched up his hat and coat.

"My entire life long I've gotten along splendidly by myself!" he said with conviction. "You have been nothing more than pebbles in my shoe! Slowing me down! Endangering my life! Making me risk everything, all I've ever lived for." Phileas fired his next statement at Passepartout. "And you knew that!" he cried.

Phileas stormed out of the house. Monique turned to Passepartout.

"Don't let him go," she said with true worry in her voice. "He'll be lost by midnight."

Passepartout had the same thought. He hurried out after Phileas, then came to a sudden stop, stunned by the sight before him.

Phileas was on his knees, surrounded by a dozen Black Scorpion agents. Their bladed weapons hovered dangerously near his neck.

13 ❖ In Which a Bad Situation Gets Worse

THE SITUATION LOOKED BAD for Phileas Fogg. The Black Scorpions locked Phileas, Monique, and Passepartout into stockades—wooden cages that confined their bodies yet left their heads exposed.

"A thousand pardons, Mr. Fogg," Passepartout said, full of guilt.

"Is there anything you've told me that's even remotely true?" a hurt and betrayed Phileas asked.

"I really can sing," Passepartout remarked, and quickly sang a verse of "Frère Jacques."

Phileas, fed up with Passepartout, turned to face Monique.

"Perhaps you should see if Prince Hapi's offer

still stands," Phileas sarcastically suggested.

Just then, a group of Black Scorpions approached, with their leader, Bak Mei. The most menacing of all of Fang's agents, he wore dragon-shaped metal gauntlets on his muscular forearms.

"Where is the jade Buddha?" Bak Mei barked at Passepartout.

"You are better off killing me," Passepartout boldly retorted.

Bak Mei didn't doubt Passepartout's bravery. "You have nerve," he said. "But are your comrades so brave?"

The Black Scorpion stalked toward Phileas, flashing his deadly gauntlet.

"Your threats don't frighten me," Phileas said. "Nor does your silly bracelet."

SHHK! A long, sharp blade emerged from the gauntlet, hovering near Phileas's throat.

"All right," Phileas said, gulping back fear. "It's not silly."

"I spit on you!" Monique screamed defiantly. "*Vive* Lanzhou!"

Bak Mei moved in close to Monique. "Your turn will come soon enough," he sneered.

Passepartout thought that threatening a

woman was the last straw. "Coward!" he called out. "Fight me!"

Bak Mei grinned ferociously. "Let's see how brave you really are," he snarled.

The Black Scorpions unlocked Passepartout's stockade. Passepartout leaped out, poised and ready for the impending fight. The other Black Scorpions formed a circle around the two combatants, bracing for the battle.

Passepartout fought Bak Mei heroically, with a dazzling display of kung fu kicks and punches. Phileas was amazed. He had never seen this side of his valet before. Bak Mei was no match for Passepartout's lightning-fast moves. He quickly called out for the other Black Scorpions' help.

Soon, Passepartout was battling not one, but a dozen Black Scorpions, all by himself! It was too much for a single man to handle—every time he got the upper hand, one of the Black Scorpions would attack him from behind.

"They're cheating!" Monique shouted.

"Yes," Phileas said ironically. "You don't expect that from ruthless killers."

"Passepartout, behind you!" Monique shouted as a Black Scorpion moved in. "Look out!"

With Monique's help, Passepartout evaded his attackers and even tricked them into hitting each other. Suddenly, Passepartout was beating a half dozen Black Scorpions all by himself!

"Silence her!" Bak Mei ordered. He was battered and bruised. A soldier covered Monique's head with a sack. With Monique temporarily sightless, Phileas tried to guide Passepartout, but the speed of the fighting left him confused.

"Punching man approaching," he warned Passepartout. "Watch out on the right!"

Passepartout threw a flying kick to the right, but there was nobody there. Before he could recover his bearings, Passepartout took a devastating kick to the chest from a Black Scorpion agent who was actually to his left.

"I meant *my* right! Sorry!" Phileas shouted.

"Mr. Fogg, stop helping me!" Passepartout called out desperately.

It was too late. Passepartout was simply outnumbered. Bak Mei finished him off with a series of kicks, knocking him into the back of the cart before sending it rolling down a hill.

The Black Scorpions laughed as Passepartout struggled to free himself from the runaway cart.

Just as it was about to smash into a hut, a mysterious, hooded man grabbed the cart, bringing the vehicle to a sudden stop.

"What took you so long?" a dazed Passepartout asked.

"I had to finish my lunch!" explained the mysterious man—removing his mask. It was none other than Wong Fei Hung.

"Wong Fei Hung! Surely you are not foolish enough to take on all my men by yourself?" Bak Mei sneered.

Wong Fei Hung smiled mischievously. "Who said I was alone?"

Eight more masked fighters, all dressed in black, sprang from trees, dived out of buildings, leaped off rooftops—each one more fearsome than the next.

"Get the Ten Tigers!" shouted Bak Mei.

The two sides clashed.

No matter how many Black Scorpions attacked, the Ten Tigers beat them back with a dazzling array of kicks and punches.

Incensed, Bak Mei gave a new order. "Execute the prisoners!" he commanded. Bak Mei and two of his men dashed over to Phileas and Monique, swords raised.

But then, Passepartout rushed to the rescue, overpowering the two agents just in time to save Phileas and Monique. He turned and finished Bak Mei off with a devastating kick that sent his antagonist somersaulting through the air.

When Bak Mei looked up, he realized that none of his men were still standing. Their beaten bodies were scattered everywhere. The Ten Tigers, however, were all still standing. They closed in on him.

"You promise me the Black Scorpions will never come back to Lanzhou!" Passepartout demanded.

Bak Mei nodded fearfully in agreement, running off to safety.

Passepartout turned to Phileas and Monique. "These are my brothers and sisters: The Ten Tigers," he declared.

"They're real," Phileas said in amazement. "The legend was true."

The Black Scorpions having been defeated, Passepartout, Wong Fei Hung, and the other Tigers placed the sacred jade Buddha back in the village temple, where it belonged.

It was a great moment for the village of

Lanzhou. However, Passepartout's worries were not over. He watched as Phileas prepared to leave the village. . . . by himself.

"Mr. Fogg, I am so sorry," Passepartout said.

"Passepartout, or whatever your name is, save your apologies," Phileas said stubbornly.

"Phileas, he risked his life for what he believes in," Monique explained. "If anyone understands that, you should."

Phileas ignored her pleas. "Please ensure that Miss Larouche finds safe passage home," he said, handing Passepartout a roll of banknotes. "This should be adequate."

"Mr. Fogg. Please let us help you win your bet," Passepartout begged. But Phileas refused to consider it.

Phileas Fogg climbed atop an ox-driven cart bound for the Chinese coast and continued on his daring world journey . . . alone.

14 ❖ In Which Phileas Runs Out of Luck

THE CLOCK WAS TICKING. By the time Phileas reached San Francisco, he had only nineteen days left to win his bet.

Though he was alone, he was still confident. He would win his wager with Lord Kelvin even without the help of Passepartout and Monique. After all, he had just traversed China and the Pacific Ocean on his own. He stepped off the ship onto Fisherman's Wharf, his confidence boosted.

"Ahhh, San Francisco—the most modern city in the world," he said, savoring the images of trolley cars and electric lights. "Finally—civilization."

San Francisco was modern. But it was also a city with rough edges. The city had been formed during the Gold Rush. At heart, it was still an Old West frontier town. And many people—especially along the docks—were untrustworthy.

Phileas's plan was to take the railroad east to New York. None of the people he asked, however, would give him directions to the Pacific Railroad Station.

In addition to being the most modern city in the world, San Francisco was also the rudest, Phileas thought. A beautiful woman in a red dress suddenly ran smack into him, jarring him and knocking herself and him both to the ground.

"I'm so sorry," she said as she tried to get up.

"It's my fault entirely," he said, helping her.

He started to help the woman to her feet, but she grimaced and let out a cry of pain.

"I think I've sprained my knee!" she whimpered.

"Maybe you should elevate your leg?"

"Thanks," she said, wincing as Phileas lifted her leg and propped it on his bag of money.

"You need a physician," he said, helpfully.

The beautiful woman nodded. "There's a kind old doctor who has an office just around the corner," she said, and motioned down the street.

"Excellent!" he replied. "I'll get him for you."

He dashed off in search of the doctor.

"Thank you so much!" she called after him. "There should be more people like you in the world!" Once he was out of earshot, though she added: "Rich and stupid!"

When she was sure Phileas was out of sight, the woman hopped up onto her feet and grabbed his bag. She wasn't hurt at all. She was just one of the many unsavory characters working the docks. By the time Phileas returned, the woman—and all of his money and belongings—were gone.

15 ❖ In Which Fang Turns on Fogg

Lord Kelvin was relaxing comfortably in his private office at the Royal Academy when General Fang paid him an unexpected visit.

"I'm sorry to say that the jade Buddha has been returned to Lanzhou," she informed him. "It is to be protected in perpetuity by the Ten Tigers."

Kelvin was furious. As he did in times of anger, he reached for a quill. "Consider our deal—"

Before he could finish, Fang grabbed his hand, placing the quill back in its holder.

"I can offer you something much more precious than a single jade Buddha," she promised.

Lord Kelvin sat back down. He was curious to learn more. Fang stepped over to a wall map of

China and continued with her idea.

"Beneath Lanzhou are a series of untapped jade reserves," she explained, pointing to specific areas on the map. "If the town were to be overrun, those reserves would be mine—I mean, *ours*."

Kelvin finally realized why Fang had wanted to control Lanzhou all along. The priceless Buddha she had once stolen for him was nothing compared with all the money she would make from owning those jade mines. She had tricked him, and he was impressed.

"It seems, General Fang, that you are not only a ruthless warlord, but an astute businesswoman, as well," he said, calculating the information in his mind. "I'm starting to like you. However . . ." he reminded her, "should Phileas Fogg win this race, I will have neither the power nor the means to hand over any arsenal."

"Then I will see to it personally that Mr. Fogg's trip is cut short," Fang asserted. She would stop Phileas Fogg all by herself.

16 ❖ IN WHICH THE TRIO IS REUNITED

IF LORD KELVIN HAD HAD ANY IDEA of how Fogg's trip had really been going, he wouldn't have been worried at all. The inventor had lost not only all of his clothing and money, but all of his hope as well. He was certain that he would never make it to London in time to win the bet.

Once a proper English gentleman with visions of running the Royal Academy, Phileas was now reduced to begging for money on a muddy street in San Francisco. And he clearly didn't possess the skills to do that well.

Upon watching Phileas repeatedly fail to get any change, a hobo gave him pointers on how to beg properly.

"You just gotta figure out what'll work for you," the unkempt man told him. "Now, what makes you different from them?" he asked, pointing at the well-off people walking past.

"I'm hungry and miserable," Phileas said.

"Keep going," said the hobo.

"My clothes smell," Phileas added.

"You're getting warmer," the hobo said.

Phileas pondered. "I smell?" he tried.

The hobo shook his head. "No, you *stink*! And your stink is your most powerful weapon. People *fear* stink! Now, watch this—"

The man stopped a passerby and stuck out his hand. "Give me some money, or I'll poop my pants!"

Frightened, the pedestrian tossed some coins at the hobo and hurried along. Having no better ideas of his own, Phileas gave the routine a try.

Phileas approached the next pedestrian, his voice quivering somewhat. "Give me some of that money, or else I shall poop in my pants!" he said.

The man considered Phileas's request for a moment—and then punched him in the face.

"Ouch," said the hobo sympathetically. "I'm not going to lie to you. That's going to happen about half the time. It's a volume business."

Dejected, Phileas staggered back to the gutter and sat down. Beside him rested his only remaining possession—his notebook. He flipped through it, coming across an unexpected sight—Monique's sketch of the sunrise they had seen from the Orient Express. She had added a flying man to the sketch, just like the one in her painting in the gallery.

Phileas stared at the drawing of the beautiful sunrise, moved by its beauty. He turned it over and noticed an inscription scrawled on the back. It read, *I traveled the world for inspiration and found it in a man who lives what he dreams*.

The thought of Monique brought tears to his eyes. He had lost everything—even her. He glanced up at the people passing by on the street and was shocked when one of them stopped, seeming to recognize him.

"Phileas?" said the woman.

Phileas couldn't believe his eyes. It was Monique—and Passepartout was by her side!

"Monique! Passepartout!" he cried, not able to believe his eyes. "You crossed the Pacific Ocean for me?"

Monique smiled warmly at Phileas. "We

will help you win your bet."

Passepartout added, "Mr. Fogg, I will never let you down!"

Phileas was touched to think that they had come searching for him. "But why have you done this?"

"Because you are our friend," Monique said. Then she smiled and added, "And perhaps more."

"More with her, maybe," Passepartout added. "You and me, we'll just stay friends."

Phileas hugged them both tightly.

Only then did his friends get a good whiff of him. The hobo was right, he stank. Passepartout and Monique winced at the odor.

"What happened to you?" Monique asked.

"You smell really bad," added Passepartout.

"I'm afraid I've been robbed!" Phileas admitted. "Rendered penniless!"

Monique smiled. "You're no longer penniless. Remember that money you gave Passepartout to get rid of me?"

Passepartout smiled as he held up the wad of cash Phileas had given him in China.

"We can do it, Phileas!" Monique cried.

There was no time to spare. They had sixteen days to travel from San Francisco to London.

17 ❖ IN WHICH THE TRAVELERS ARE THIRSTY

DRESSED IN FULL COWBOY GEAR, the trio traveled east from San Francisco by stagecoach. Along the way, they saw gold-mining towns, farming villages, a new country growing from the wilderness.

Now, they were stuck in the most accurately named place in all of America—Death Valley.

It was a searing desert, completely barren of any living thing except for cactuses and the vultures that circled the skies waiting for any poor souls that might have chosen this place to die.

It was an unfortunate spot for one of the wheels of their stagecoach to break. Passepartout nobly offered to trudge through the blistering desert to look for help.

After he had been gone for some time, Monique grew worried.

"It's been hours since Passepartout went to get help," she said, weakly raising her canteen to take a drink of water, only to find that it was empty.

"Don't fret, my dear," Phileas said, confidently. "Passepartout is a keen warrior with impeccable survival instincts. I have no doubt he will return with help, and we will board our train in Reno with time to spare."

Despite Phileas's confidence, Passepartout was not having much luck. He had lost his way, his canteen, and his mind. Drenched in sweat, he collapsed on the sandy ground, delirious from the heat. He rolled over, to find himself face to face with a steer's skull that had been picked clean by the buzzards and bleached white by the relentless sun.

What a beautiful woman, Passepartout thought in his confusion. He began kissing it.

Back at the stagecoach, Phileas moved quickly from slight concern to full-fledged panic.

"Help! Help us!" Phileas ranted. "I don't want to die!"

A pair of young men rode up in a horse-drawn

carriage. Embarrassed, Phileas tried to regain his composure.

"Howdy," he said, trying to sound like an actual cowboy.

"Hey, crazy English cowboy wannabe man," one of the men said, mocking Phileas. "Go be crazy somewhere else! You're blocking the trail!"

The other man, however, recognized Phileas right away.

"Wilbur, it's him," he said as he jumped down from the carriage. The two men were Orville and Wilbur Wright, bicycle repairmen and, like Phileas, amateur inventors.

"Mr. Fogg, my name is Orville Wright," the man said, introducing himself. "This is my brother, Wilbur. We're big fans of yours."

"Fan is a strong word," Wilbur said. "Better way to say it is, we got a lot of money on you to win your bet."

"We're going to use our winnings to build this!" Orville proclaimed, showing Phileas some schematic drawings.

Phileas studied one for a moment. He realized that it was a diagram of a flying machine.

"You've got to forgive my brother," Wilbur

said. "He's got his head up in the clouds. He's one of these sad dreamers who think that one day man's going to swoosh around the planet like a hummingbird."

Phileas was humbled and impressed by the invention. The two men seemed to have improved upon his failed design.

"He's mastered the cable steering system!" Phileas marveled. "The drag and lift ratio! This is brilliant!"

"Thank you," Orville beamed.

Hearing that Phileas thought the drawings were good, Wilbur suddenly changed his tune. "That's what I've been saying," he chimed in. "You've got to have faith, no matter how crazy your brother's dreams sound."

"Excuse me, gentlemen," Monique interrupted, getting to the real issue at hand. "Have you come across our friend on your way here?"

They thought for a moment. "You mean, a crazy, half-naked Chinese guy singing 'Frère Jacques'?" Wilbur asked.

"With a cow skull on his head?" Orville added.

Phileas thought about the description for a moment. "Possibly."

"He's in the back of our wagon," Wilbur said.

Monique rushed over and opened the carriage door. There was Passepartout, giddy from too much sun, wearing his beloved cow's skull.

"Passepartout! Thank goodness, you're alive!" she shouted in glee.

Now that the group was back together, Phileas was eager to move on. "Gentlemen, could you possibly assist us with our transportation?" he asked them.

The bicycle repairmen had the perfect solution for the stranded travelers. In no time, the stagecoach was back and running, a giant bicycle wheel having replaced the broken wagon wheel. Phileas was back in the race!

18 ❖ IN WHICH THE VILLAINS REAPPEAR

THE BICYCLE-WHEELED STAGECOACH carried Phileas, Passepartout, and Monique all the way to Reno, where they boarded the Union Pacific Railroad eastbound. The train climbed into the majestic Rockies, carrying the group through snowcapped mountain peaks and across the Great Plains, where thundering herds of buffalo ran alongside the locomotive.

Phileas couldn't believe how far he'd traveled from the limiting confines of the Fogg mansion. He'd seen much of the world. His eyes had been opened to a whole new array of experiences. The journey itself had been a challenge, but Phileas was grateful to Monique for teaching him to appreciate the less scientific aspects of the world around him.

He was brimming with ideas for new inventions—things he would commence working on as soon as he returned to his home laboratory.

According to his calculations, they would reach London just in time to win the bet—but there could not be any more delays.

With eight days left, they arrived in New York, the largest city in the Americas.

They were stunned by the crowds of people that had massed to cheer them on. Word of Phileas's race had spread across the world, inspiring millions. People had gathered to show their support for the cause and to see if the trio could catch their ship to London in time.

"Our steamer for England leaves in ten minutes!" Phileas panted, glancing at his watch.

They turned a corner, running smack into another group of cheering fans. The crowd was so big that it blocked their way to the ship.

"We're never going to make it," Monique shouted above the noise of the crowd.

The trio were approached by a New York policeman, a Wanted poster clutched in his hand.

Surely, now, they were doomed.

"Phileas Fogg," he said sternly. Then he flashed a smile, "Would you autograph this for me?"

"Certainly," a relieved Phileas replied. He scribbled his name across the poster.

The ship's horn blasted, announcing the steamer's imminent departure. "The ship!" Monique cried.

The policeman had a solution. "Follow me. I know a shortcut."

He cleared a way through the crowd, leading the trio into a giant warehouse filled with crates and scaffolds. Passepartout was startled by a huge metal head that loomed behind him.

"That's a big man!" Passepartout remarked.

Monique smiled. She knew exactly what it was. Those were the giant pieces of the Statue of Liberty. It had been a gift to America from the people of France, and it was about to be assembled in New York Harbor.

"It is a lady," Monique clarified, admiring the beautiful statue. "A *French* lady!"

"She looks like an evil Chinese warlord to me," Phileas said.

Confused, Monique and Passepartout turned

to Phileas. They saw that he was referring to General Fang, who was lurking behind them.

Fang tossed a sack of coins to the policeman, who snatched them and pocketed the bribe.

"I'll be sure to lock the door from the outside," the officer said snidely, as he left the building.

"Your journey has caused a stir around the world, Mr. Fogg," Fang hissed. "But it ends here."

Passepartout shielded his friends from the general. "Leave them alone," he shouted. "This has nothing to do with them."

"On the contrary," Fang revealed. "Lord Kelvin and I have made new arrangements to conquer Lanzhou. Unfortunately for Mr. Fogg, they entail his *permanent* detour."

Five Black Scorpion agents emerged from the shadows, flanking their general. In Lanzhou, Passepartout had had the aid of the other Ten Tigers. Here, he would have to fend the agents off all by himself.

He exploded into motion, snatching a suitcase and hat bag and twirling. The weighted bags became instant weapons. One smacked a Black Scorpion in the head. Passepartout confronted the other agents, stalling them long enough for

Phileas and Monique to start climbing the scaffolding up the front of the Statue of Liberty.

"Stop them!" Fang yelled as she spotted the fleeing duo.

Passepartout continued battling the agents. Clothes flew in every direction as the suitcases-turned-shields spilled open.

As for Phileas and Monique, they encountered one dead end after another as they tried to scale the statue. Black Scorpions climbed the outside of the scaffolding, forcing Monique and Phileas into the head of the statue. Phileas became wedged in Lady Liberty's nose, where, ironically, he experienced a sudden sneezing fit.

In the distance, the horn of the steamship sounded, echoing throughout the immense warehouse. "We're going to miss the ship," Phileas realized with panic.

But Passepartout refused to let that happen. "Up there!" he shouted, spotting a skylight escape route above them. "Hurry! You must defeat Kelvin!" He stayed behind, fending off the attacking general and her agents.

Safe on the roof, Phileas was overcome with pangs of guilt. With Passepartout's life in danger, winning the bet suddenly felt less important.

"What am I thinking?" he said to Monique. "He can't defeat them all by himself—he's nine Tigers short!"

"But, Phileas, you'll lose everything if you miss your boat!" Monique reminded him.

"Not everything," Phileas remarked, touching her face gently.

Monique smiled. "I do believe you are becoming the man of my dreams," she said, deeply moved by his devotion to his friend.

They shared a smile and, hand in hand, raced back into the warehouse to help Passepartout.

A weary Passepartout dispatched the last of Fang's agents. But the general herself closed in for the kill. She took a deadly swipe at him with her sword, but he evaded her just in time. The sword cut through a nearby rope, loosening its hold on a giant bronze book.

The enormous book teetered perilously above them, threatening to flatten them.

"The book!" Monique screamed to Phileas. "It's going to fall!"

"I will save him!" Phileas shouted bravely, as he jumped to Passepartout's rescue. It was a clumsy jump, sending Phileas bouncing and tumbling down the side of the statue. But he landed right by his friend's side.

He reached for Passepartout's outstretched hand, but it was too late. The book was falling. Passepartout pushed Phileas clear, having no time to get to safety himself. The massive book slammed down on both him and General Fang. The impact sent a thundering echo through the warehouse.

Phileas stared at the fallen book, devastated. Certainly, Passepartout could not have survived such an impact.

Suddenly, Passepartout dragged himself out from beneath the book. The statue's bronze hand had created just enough space for him to shelter under and avoid being crushed.

"Passepartout! You're alive!" Phileas exclaimed.

Though he was glad that Phileas had come back to help him, Passepartout was occupied with greater concerns. "Mr. Fogg, you missed your ship! You'll lose your bet."

Phileas looked him in the eye. "At least I did not lose a friend."

Behind them, General Fang crawled out from under the book and drew back her sword, preparing to stop both men with a single blow.

The sword was suddenly knocked out of her hand by Monique's hatbox. Fang whirled to find Monique perched behind her. Inspired by the moves of the Ten Tigers, Monique then delivered a punch that knocked General Fang out cold.

The men were stunned.

"Monique, you must be the Eleventh Tiger," Passepartout joked.

"Meow!" Monique replied, catlike.

She crossed over to her traveling companions. "We must catch the next ship!" she said.

Phileas shook his head. "Pointless. It would never reach London in time."

Passepartout refused to listen to such talk. "No, no, no!" he shouted. "We are not giving up! I almost died! You almost died! We're taking the next ship to win that bet!"

Monique and Phileas were impressed.

"Very well," Phileas responded, his eyes glinting with renewed adventure. "Let's go!"

19 ❖ In Which a Bold Experiment Is Attempted

THE SUN ROSE as the steamship *Carmen* slowly made its way across the Atlantic. As he did every morning, Phileas marked off another day on the first page of his notebook. This was the seventy-sixth sunrise they had faced since leaving London, and no matter how many times he tried to recalculate his journey, he was certain they were going to run out of mornings before making it back.

"It's hopeless!" Phileas bellowed as he rechecked his figures. "By these calculations, I'm still behind by one day!"

"There must be some way!" Monique said.

Just then, the steamship captain approached, intrigued.

"Phileas? Phileas Fogg on my boat?" the captain marveled. "What an honor, sir! I've quite a penny wagered on you."

The three smiled. They had an ally.

The captain vowed to help Phileas win his bet in any way that he could. Now, all they needed was a plan.

Back at the Royal Academy, Kelvin anxiously awaited word of Phileas's progress.

The door to his office swung open. In staggered Inspector Fix—beaten, battered, and bruised. His nose was bandaged, scars covering his face.

"My goodness!" cried an amazed Colonel Kitchner. "He made it around the world."

Inspector Fix was in no mood for banter. "I came back from India the short way, ya ninny!" he barked.

Lord Kelvin studied the disheveled policeman. "I take it you don't have Phileas Fogg in that valise."

Inspector Fix shook his head no.

"A little jade Buddha, perhaps?" he asked.

Again, Inspector Fix shook his head.

"Inspector Fix, would you be so good as to

take a look at Big Ben and tell me what time it is?" Lord Kelvin asked slyly.

"Half past twelve, sir," he answered.

"Please," Lord Kelvin implored. "Look closer."

Inspector Fix was not sure what was going on, but he moved over to the window and looked toward the giant clock at the House of Parliament.

"It's definitely half past—"

Before the inspector could finish, Lord Kelvin shoved him out the window. He flailed helplessly, landing in a trash bin with a mighty thud.

On the deck of the *Carmen*, the dejected captain approached Phileas. "Mr. Fogg, I'm sorry to say we've burned the last of the coal. But I've had a word with the crew, and all of them have agreed to burn their shoes. Because individually, and as a group, we care about you." The captain gave Phileas a hearty and heartfelt hug.

"The effort is appreciated," Phileas replied. "Unfortunately, we're not even close. We've gained a mere six hours. Even shoes cannot help us now."

They all stood quietly on the deck, mourning

Phileas's losing the race. Phileas looked up. He noticed a flock of seagulls circling overhead.

"That's it!" Phileas cried out, in a burst of inspiration. "Birds!"

The captain smiled. "Excellent idea! We'll burn birds!"

"No, we'll fly to London," Phileas explained. "We'll simply follow the laws of physics mastered by the birds over millennia, and combine it with our discovery of the perfect airfoil." He turned to the captain, who looked intrigued.

"I'm afraid I have to ask your permission to dismantle this ship to build a flying machine," Phileas admitted.

The captain thought for a moment, and, with a look of determination, turned to one of his crewmen. "Cornelius, fetch me my tool kit!"

Soon, everyone on board was pitching in to help construct the flying machine. Crewmen ripped wood from the deck; others chopped down the mast as though it were a giant tree. Passepartout swung from the rigging like a pirate, cutting slices from the sail to fashion into wings.

Phileas carefully began to assemble his long-dreamed-of flying machine. The front of a lifeboat became the nose of the aircraft, sails were stretched across a wooden frame to make the wings, and steering cables were attached to the captain's wheel. It was a crazy assemblage of parts, but by the time the sun set in the horizon, it was complete.

And Phileas knew that when the sun rose the following morning, he would risk everything and take to the skies. He only hoped that he wouldn't, as he had in his dreams, come crashing down.

20 ❖ In Which the Travelers Risk Their Lives

THE *CARMEN* SPUTTERED ALONG as best it could in its dismantled state, just barely seaworthy. Passepartout stood on the ship's deck and looked out toward England.

Phileas approached with a happy bounce in his step. "Good morning," he said. "Have you seen Monique?"

Passepartout smiled and motioned across the deck. Phileas turned, amazed by what he saw. Monique had painted the flying machine so that it now looked almost like a work of Impressionist art. There were splashes of color everywhere. It was magical.

"It's glorious," Phileas said, nearly speechless. "You've obviously found your inspiration!"

And indeed, Monique had. Phileas was her inspiration. Now his dream, her artistry, and Passepartout's resourcefulness had come together in the painting of the giant contraption.

They climbed aboard the craft, taking their seats in chairs they had removed from the dining room. Phileas made one last set of calculations.

"Greenwich mean time," he said, setting his pocket watch one hour ahead, to London time. "The last time I will set my watch ahead."

He took a deep breath and turned to the others. "Well, shall we fly?"

Monique and Passepartout beamed with excitement. They nodded. They seemed ready to take off.

"Godspeed, Mr. Fogg," the captain called out to them.

"Thank you," Phileas replied. Then he shouted out, "Prepare for takeoff!"

"Yes, sir!" Passepartout answered and began to pedal what looked like a bicycle. The pedals were connected to a chain, which turned gears and brought the propeller to life. The faster

Passepartout moved his feet, the faster the propeller spun.

"Tallyho!" Phileas shouted.

Using the mast, the crew had constructed a giant bow across the front of the deck. A rope was cinched back, tightening the mast until it would move no further. A crewman brought down an ax, chopping through the rope that was holding the mast back. Its tension released, the wooden pole sprang forward—rocketing the flying machine up a ramp and off the front of the ship.

The flying machine rose high into the air in an arc, soaring into the clouds. From the ship below, the crewmen cheered, thrilled that this experiment was working.

Passepartout moved his feet as fast as he could as the machine reached the top of its arc.

Just as it was about to head back down, Phileas shouted to Monique: "Now!"

Monique pulled back on Phileas's cane, which had been turned into a lever. The wings snapped out to their full extension and caught the wind, lifting the aircraft. They steadied their course and were carried forward.

"You did it, Phileas!" Monique exulted. "We

are flying!" She closed her eyes and enjoyed the rush of the wind against her face.

Passepartout stared out at the horizon, amazed.

Phileas had to keep reminding himself that it wasn't one of his dreams. It was really happening.

"My God!" Phileas declared. "It's . . . perfect!"

"Yes," Monique agreed. "Your calculations, this invention. It's flawless."

"Not the machine," Phileas said, correcting her. "Flying!"

"Better than your dreams?" she asked.

Phileas beamed as he savored it all. "Better than my dreams!"

Thrilled to be part of making his dreams a reality, Monique reached forward and wrapped her arms around Phileas. Phileas steered the craft, banking through the clouds and on toward England.

21 ◆ In Which a Dream Comes True

PASSEPARTOUT MOVED HIS FEET with all his might. Exhausted, he looked through a bank of clouds and saw something that gave him a great boost.

"Land ho!" he bellowed.

Phileas looked through his trusty telescope. "Cornwall!" he confirmed. "The south coast of England."

They were close, but would they make it in time? According to the rules laid out in the bet, Phileas had to reach the top step of the Royal Academy before Big Ben struck noon.

Inside the Royal Academy, Lord Kelvin was sulking. He had just received a telegram from General Fang saying that Phileas and the others had eluded her in New York.

Kelvin's assistant burst into his office with unbelievable news. "A flying machine is headed for the Royal Academy," the assistant cried breathlessly. "Witnesses swear it's Phileas Fogg at the controls!"

Lord Kelvin let forth a ferocious roar.

Up in the skies, the flying machine began its descent to London. A steering cable suddenly snapped, the wing fluttered uncontrollably. The three travelers screamed as the craft quickly began losing altitude.

"Oh, dear," Phileas cried. "Unfortunately, this is *exactly* like my dream."

"I'm going to retrieve it," Passepartout shouted as he climbed along the wing to grab the cable. He reached it successfully, but then another cable snapped. The flying machine did not look as though it would stay together much longer.

All over London, people looked up from the streets to see an unbelievable sight—Phileas Fogg, flying to victory!

Kelvin exited the Royal Academy just in time to see Phileas and his flying machine heading right toward him. "Get the police here, now!" he instructed Colonel Kitchner. "I want Fogg arrested the moment his feet touch British soil!"

Kitchner blew his police whistle, putting the call out for bobbies.

As the flying machine plummeted toward London, the crowds scattered out of the way.

The machine slammed to the ground, hitting the street in a shower of sparks and skidding to a halt at the bottom steps of the Royal Academy.

The crowd erupted in cheers that ended abruptly when Kelvin stepped forward, surrounded by bobbies.

"Arrest them!" he ordered. "They robbed the Bank of England!"

The bobbies grabbed Phileas, Passepartout, and Monique. Unable to move, Phileas was a few feet from the steps when Big Ben struck noon.

He had lost the bet.

"Noon!" said Passepartout dejectedly.

"We did our best," Phileas said, trying to put on a brave face.

"Outta me way!" a cockney voice cried. "Move it!" The crowd parted to reveal the beaten, battered Inspector Fix.

"Get this buffoon out of here," Lord Kelvin bellowed.

"Buffoon?" Inspector Fix said. "That's the thanks I get after going halfway around the world to stop Fogg for you?"

Suddenly the crowd started buzzing with the news that they had just heard—Kelvin had cheated.

The mob began to turn on Kelvin, but he was defiant. "Oh, boo-hoo!" he said, mocking the people. "So what if I did try to stop Phileas Fogg? What are you gutless peons going to do about it? I hold all the power. I run everything—the railway, the horse trade. I'm the reason your undergarments are made of a wool/cotton blend."

The crowd was stunned by Kelvin's blatant confession of guilt.

"So, which of you half-wits is going to stop me?" he asked.

"The queen," announced a little girl in the front row.

"That antiquated old cow?" Kelvin scoffed. "The only way she could stop me is if she sat on me with her big, fat, royal bottom!"

The crowd stood in stunned silence. A frightening thought struck Kelvin. "She's behind me, isn't she?" he asked.

The other lords nodded as Kelvin turned to find himself face to face with Queen Victoria.

"Your Majesty," Kelvin said, trying to smooth things over. "I have just apprehended the culprits who robbed the Bank of England."

Phileas, Passepartout, and Monique started to plead their case. The crowd joined in.

"Quiet!" Queen Victoria barked. The entire crowd instantly became silent.

"I love being able to do that," she gloated. "So, Lord Kelvin," she said in a pointed tone. "Unsportsmanlike conduct, attempted murder, trading my arsenal for Buddhas?"

"I assure you, there's an explanation for all of this," Kelvin stammered, trying to come up with one. His mind blank, all he could think to do was run. And he did.

A swarm of bobbies quickly gave chase, quickly capturing and cuffing him and then throwing him in the back of the police wagon. The crowd cheered as Kelvin was driven off to prison.

Queen Victoria approached Phileas. "So this is Phileas Fogg's miraculous flying invention?" she asked, pointing to the wreckage of the machine.

"Your Majesty, we all invented it," Phileas said, motioning to Passepartout and Monique.

"But we failed to help Phileas win his bet," a saddened Monique whispered. "I'm sorry."

"Don't be," Phileas said. "I saw the world! I learned of new cultures! I flew across the ocean! I wore women's clothing!"

Queen Victoria and everyone else exchanged curious looks.

"I made a friend," Phileas continued, looking at Passepartout. "I fell in love," he said, remembering as he gazed over at Monique. "Who cares if I lost a wager?"

"I do!" said the queen. "I've bet twenty quid on you!"

"But, Your Highness," said Phileas sadly. "It is already past noon."

"Correct. Which gives you twenty-four hours!" she stated.

"Could we have miscounted?" asked Monique.

Phileas recalled his journey—as they traveled east, they had moved their watches ahead one hour for each time zone—losing an hour each time.

"The international date line," Phileas shouted.

"We set our watches forward at twenty-four time zones! So, here in London, it is still day seventy-nine!"

Phileas, Monique, and Passepartout hugged one another and jumped up and down in excitement. The bet had not been lost. They still had an entire day to spare.

"Go and win your bet, Mr. Fogg," Queen Victoria said, motioning toward the steps of the Royal Academy. "I shall need a new minister of science!"

The three world travelers locked arms and marched to the top step of the Royal Academy in victory.

"We won!" Monique cried, thrilled, when they arrived.

Phileas savored the moment as he looked down at the cheering crowd, the queen, and the wreckage of his flying machine.

He took Monique into his arms and gave her a long, deep kiss, then raised his arms in victory. With the help of his friends, he had succeeded.

Phileas Fogg had traveled around the world in eighty days!

BONUS
FACTS

AROUND THE WORLD IN 80 DAYS: THEN AND NOW

The new big screen adventure *Around the World in 80 Days* is based on an 1873 novel by French writer Jules Verne (1828–1905). While the new film is different from the original novel in many ways, it was inspired by many of the same ideas that fired Verne's imagination. Verne was fascinated with progress and with the discoveries of the late nineteenth century, when train and steamship travel were first invented, along with the telephone and telegraph systems, as well as the lightbulb, among many others. Verne's time also saw advances in connecting areas of the world, namely the completion of the national railways in America and India and the opening of the Suez Canal in 1869.

CHANGES FROM NOVEL TO SCREEN

Verne's original novel was set in 1873, while this version is set in the late nineteenth century. In the novel, Passepartout really was French, not Chinese. But, as in the new version, the original Passepartout was a fitness fanatic who relied on his strength and abilities as a gymnast to help get the travelers out of several scrapes.

Verne's Phileas Fogg was a man obsessed by schedules, who, along his journey, discovers both love and his own heroism. But Verne's Phileas was not an inventor. The new Phileas shares Verne's own passion for science and invention.

There was no Monique in the original version. Instead, there was a beautiful Indian woman named Aouda, whom Phileas rescued from death by an act of selfless courage.

Other details, too, are different, but the essence of the story remains unchanged: it is the tale of a fantastic adventure, made possible through advances in technology, in which three people team up to win a crazy bet. Along the way, they find adventure, friendship, and love, and the excitement of exploration and discovery.

AROUND THE WORLD IN 80 DAYS:
FACT AND FICTION

To create the plot of the film, we took many liberties both with Verne's original novel and with some of the dates, inventions, and events we show in the film. Of course, Verne himself and many other great storytellers did not always "stick to the facts" when telling a story. Here are some the facts that lie behind the fiction of *Around the World in 80 Days*.

THE ROYAL ACADEMY OF SCIENCE • PAGE 13

The Royal Academy is not a real place. But Great Britain is home to an organization called the Royal Society, which is housed at the National Academy of Science. The Royal Society, which was founded in 1660, is dedicated to the pursuit of scientific inquiry. Admission to the Society is very selective, and members must follow strict rules of conduct.

LORD WILLIAM THOMSON KELVIN (1824–1907) • PAGE 14

While there was a real Lord Kelvin, who was president of the Royal Society, our character is fictional. But he shares some opinions with the real Lord Kelvin, who once said in a speech, "Everything has already been invented." Lord Kelvin was a mathematician and physicist, who was responsible for the absolute scale of temperature (called the Kelvin scale) and the second law of thermodynamics.

LOUIS PASTEUR • PAGE 14

Louis Pasteur (1822–1895) was a French chemist who was responsible for many advances, including the process of pasteurization and the development of the vaccine against anthrax, which was successfully administered to cattle to protect them from rabies.

JADE • PAGE 16

Jade is the common name for either of two minerals, nephrite and jadeite, which are widely used as gems. Since 2950 B.C., jade has been treasured in China as a royal and sacred stone. It is traditionally associated with the five cardinal virtues as seen by the Chinese: charity, modesty, courage, justice, and wisdom.

QUEEN VICTORIA
(1819–1901) • PAGE 18

Queen Victoria took over the throne of Great Britain in 1837. Her long reign, sometimes called the Victorian era, corresponded with a period of rapid change and advancement in almost every area of society.

THE LIGHTBULB • PAGE 22

The lightbulb was invented in 1879 by both Thomas Edison of the United States and Sir Joseph Wilson Swan of England, based on the work of a number of scientists over the previous fifty years. There is no record of the date when "whistle on, whistle off" lightbulbs were invented.

This device, which made the horseless carriage possible, went through many stages of development after its original invention between 1680, when a gunpowder-powered engine was designed (but never built), and 1885, when the German inventor Gottlieb Daimler invented what is now considered the first modern internal combustion engine. (It was powered by gas, not beans!)

URBAN TRANSPORT DEVICES • PAGE 25

Roller skates, invented in the seventeen hundreds, were actually a familiar sight by 1885 (though in-line skates were not invented until much later). In 1760, a Londoner named Joseph Merlin shocked a crowd by scooting in to a costume party playing a violin and wearing metal-wheeled boots. Unfortunately, Merlin could not control his skates, and he ran directly into a large, mirrored wall.

IMPRESSIONISM • PAGE 42

Phileas's words, "Trees are not violet . . ." were actually spoken in 1874 by a real art critic named Albert Wolff. The Impressionists' new method of trying to capture fleeting moments in time or "first impressions" was considered revolutionary.

VINCENT VAN GOGH/
"STARRY NIGHT" • PAGE 43

Vincent van Gogh is one of the most instantly recognizable of Impressionist painters. He painted most of his most famous works during the two and a half years before he died in 1890.

THE TUILERIES • PAGE 47

This sixty-three-acre garden remains today a public park. The name comes from the tiled kilns, or *tuileries*, that previously occupied the site. Many famous movies have been filmed in this landmark park.

THE HOT-AIR BALLOON • PAGE 48

The first hot-air balloon flight was made in 1763, when Frenchman Joseph Montgolfier loaded a sheep, a rooster, and a duck into a fabric balloon and sent it up into the sky. The first balloon flight made by a human passenger took place a year later.

THE ORIENT EXPRESS • PAGE 52

In 1883, the Orient Express commenced service from Paris to Constantinople, crossing six countries, with the cooperation of ten different railroads—an amazing feat for that time period. The train was famous for its luxurious five-course meals and for its passengers, who often numbered among them, diplomats, royalty, and government couriers.

Auguste Rodin
(1840–1917) • Page 62

François-Auguste-René Rodin was one of the most celebrated sculptors of all time. He created a statue called *The Thinker* that looks a bit like the statue of Prince Hapi.

Legend of the Ten Tigers • Page 69

While rooted in truth, the legend of the "Ten Tigers of Canton" has become shrouded in mystery over the years. During the Ch'ing Dynasty (1644–1911 A.D.) the Imperial Rulers, non-Chinese northern invaders, were seen as indifferent to the plight of the common man and woman. The most famous "Tiger" was Wong Fei-Hung (1847–1924), who is widely revered by the Chinese as the "true Robin Hood." He and his method of fighting, the tiger-crane form, have been widely portrayed by actors such as Jet Li in hundreds of films and TV shows.

Agra • Page 67

The present-day city was established in 1566 by the Mughal leader Akbar. Under Shah Jahan (1628–58), Agra's crowning glory, the majestic and beautiful Taj Mahal, was built.

India under British Rule • Page 68

During the eighteen hundreds, the British Empire became the world's largest empire, controlling over 25 percent of the world's population and area and covering a total of 4 million square miles. At its peak, in the Victorian era, the British Empire included India, Australia, Canada, New Zealand, South Africa, Rhodesia, Hong Kong, Gibraltar, several islands in the West Indies, and various colonies in Africa. The British officially left India in 1948, and the nation of India became a sovereign republic in 1950.

SAN FRANCISCO • PAGE 93

San Francisco was first settled in 1776 by Spanish explorers, and it was officially claimed by the United States in 1846. San Francisco is most famous today for tourist destinations such as the Golden Gate Bridge, the former prison called Alcatraz, and Fisherman's Wharf, which is still operating.

DEATH VALLEY • PAGE 102

Death Valley is a desert in eastern California that covers more than 3 million acres of wilderness. The floor of the valley is almost 300 feet below sea level. It is recognized as the lowest point in the Western Hemisphere. Death Valley is one of the hottest places on earth; temperatures of up to 134 degrees Fahrenheit have been recorded, along with an average yearly rainfall of less than two inches.

Orville and Wilbur Wright started their inventing lives when they opened a bicycle shop in Dayton, Ohio, in 1893. Wilbur was the brother who first thought about inventing an airplane, in 1899. (Experiments in aviation were under way in many parts of the world at that time.) The Wright brothers invented a plane that made it possible for Orville Wright to take the first heavier-than-air-machine-powered flight, at Kitty Hawk, North Carolina, on December 17, 1903.

THE STATUE OF LIBERTY • PAGE 109

The Statue of Liberty was designed by the French sculptor Frédéric-Auguste Bartholdi to commemorate the friendship and alliance that had existed between the two countries since the American Revolution. It was constructed of copper sheets, and was 152 feet (46 meters) in height; and it was wholly constructed in France. It was shipped to New York City in 1885 and assembled there, and it was dedicated in 1886.

THE TRANSATLANTIC STEAMSHIP • PAGE 115

Steamship travel across the Atlantic Ocean became commonplace in the 1840s. Crossing the sea on a ship like the *Carmen* would not have been an unusual event.

Since the Wright Brothers' feat was still in the future at the time the story depicted in the film took place, Phileas, Monique, and Passepartout's dramatic return to London is fiction, not fact. But the bravery that powered the last leg of the journey was definitely in the spirit of nineteenth-century invention!